CAUGHT IN A MYSTERIOUS EXPLOSION, MILD-MANNERED DASHIELL JAMES HAS BECOME TOP NASCAR DRIVER JIMMY DASH. HIS LOYAL CREW HAS ALSO DEVELOPED SUPER POWERS AND TOGETHER THEY HAVE RISEN TO THE TOP OF THE STANDINGS. BUT JIMMY'S ARCHRIVAL JACK DIESEL HAS POWERS OF HIS OWN, AND WILL STOP AT NOTHING TO WIN.

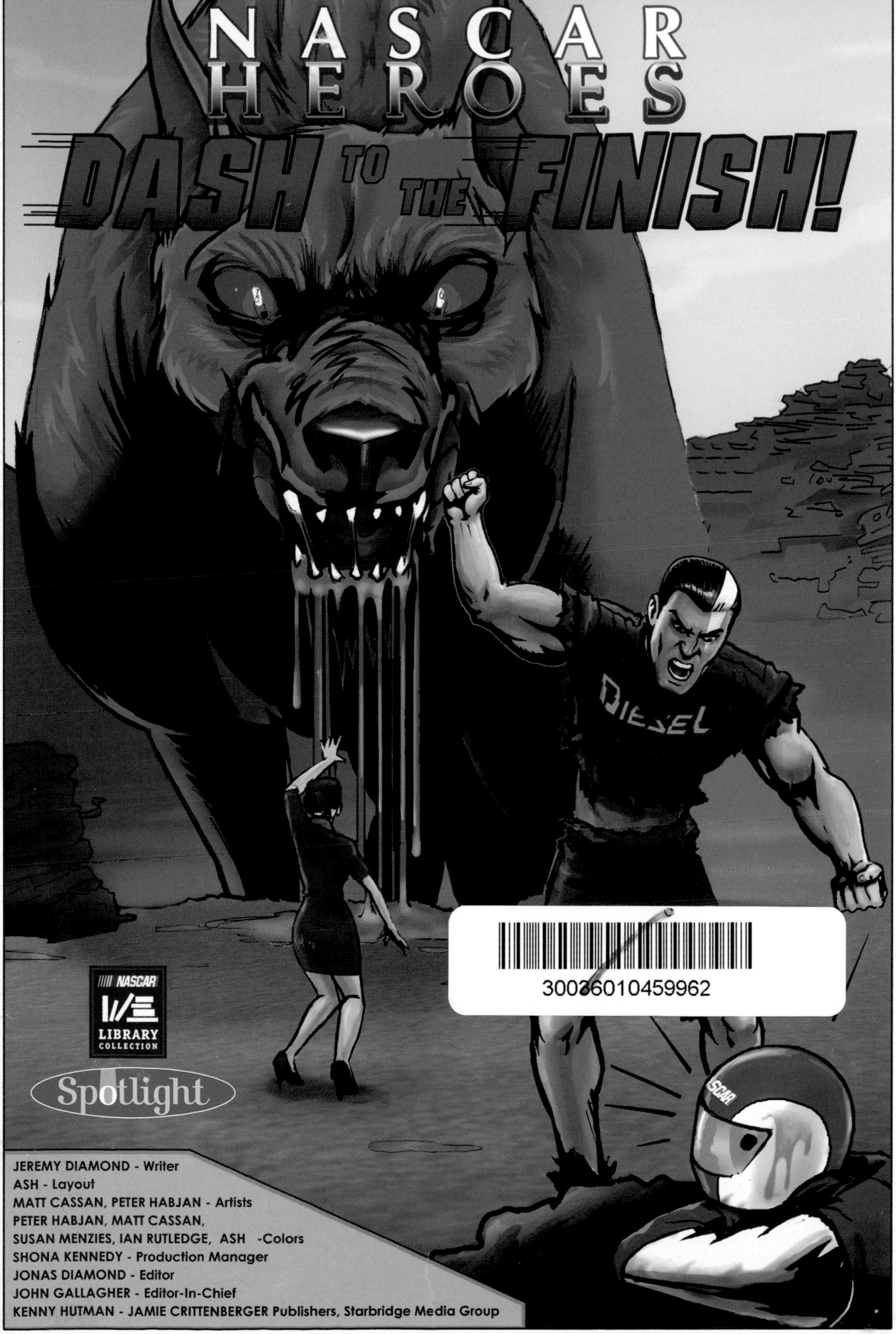
NASCAR HEROES
DASH TO THE FINISH!
DIESEL
NASCAR
LIBRARY COLLECTION
Spotlight

JEREMY DIAMOND - Writer
ASH - Layout
MATT CASSAN, PETER HABJAN - Artists
PETER HABJAN, MATT CASSAN,
SUSAN MENZIES, IAN RUTLEDGE, ASH -Colors
SHONA KENNEDY - Production Manager
JONAS DIAMOND - Editor
JOHN GALLAGHER - Editor-In-Chief
KENNY HUTMAN - JAMIE CRITTENBERGER Publishers, Starbridge Media Group

VISIT US AT
www.abdopublishing.com

Reinforced library bound edition published in 2010 by Spotlight, a division of the ABDO Group, 8000 West 78th Street, Edina, Minnesota 55439. Spotlight produces high-quality reinforced library bound editions for schools and libraries. Published by agreement with Starbridge Media Group, Inc.

Library of Congress Cataloging-in-Publication Data

Diamond, Jeremy.
  Dash to the finish! / Jeremy Diamond, writer ; Matt Cassan, Peter Habjan, artists. -- Reinforced library bound ed.
       p. cm. -- (NASCAR heroes ; #3)
  "Nascar Library Collection."
  Summary: Diesel has kidnapped Astor in hopes of preventing Jimmy Dash from driving in the next NASCAR race, but supercharged Dash and his crew have a few tricks up their sleeves to combat everything from a car crusher to a very mean dog.
  ISBN 978-1-59961-664-3
  1. Graphic novels. [1. Graphic novels. 2. Automobile racing--Fiction. 3. NASCAR (Association)--Fiction. 4. Superheroes--Fiction.] I. Cassan, Matt, ill. II. Habjan, Peter, ill. III. Title.
  PZ7.7.D52Das 2009
  741.5'973--dc22
                            2009009009

All Spotlight books have reinforced library bindings and are manufactured in the United States of

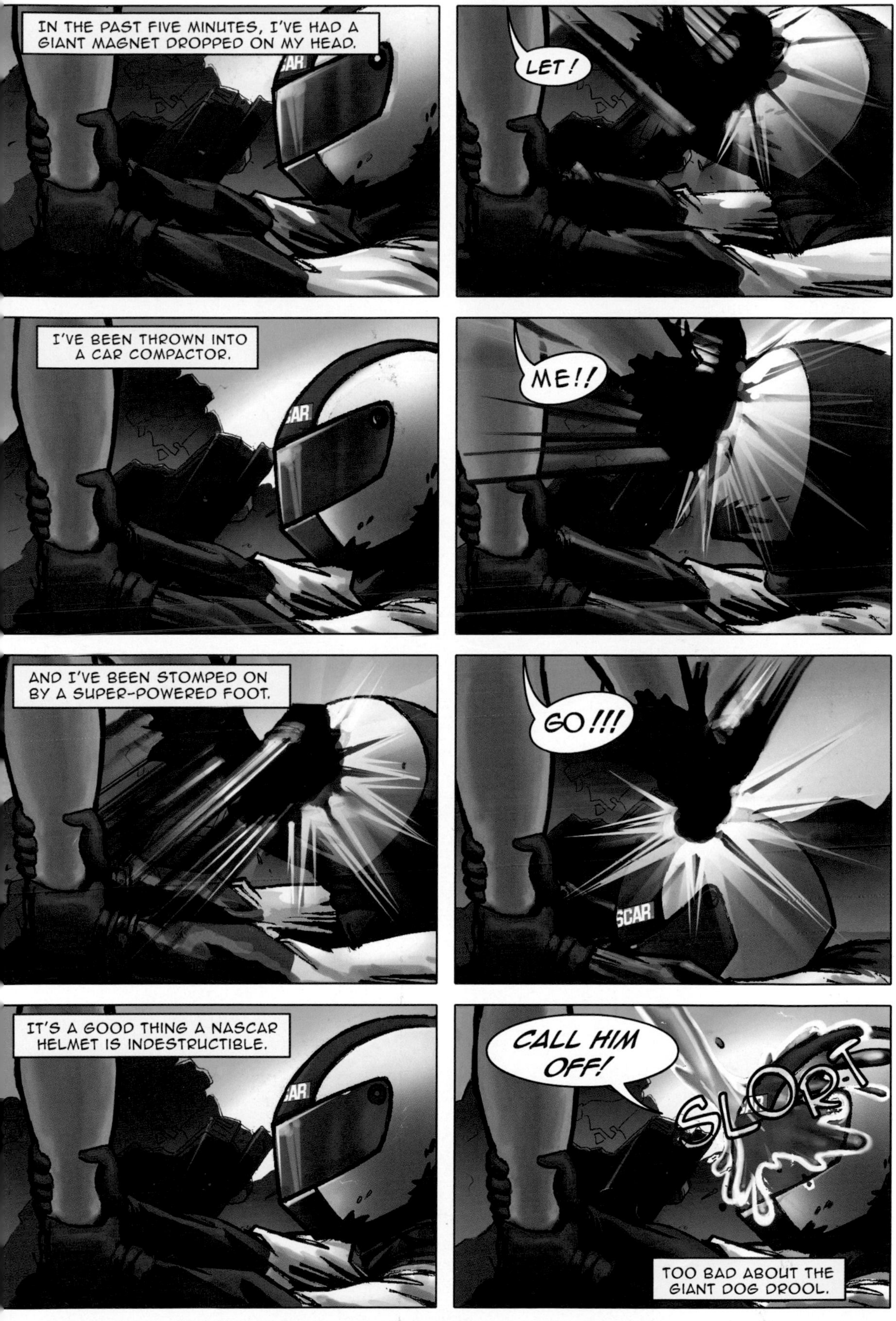
IN THE PAST FIVE MINUTES, I'VE HAD A GIANT MAGNET DROPPED ON MY HEAD.
LET!
I'VE BEEN THROWN INTO A CAR COMPACTOR.
ME!!
AND I'VE BEEN STOMPED ON BY A SUPER-POWERED FOOT.
GO!!!
IT'S A GOOD THING A NASCAR HELMET IS INDESTRUCTIBLE.
CALL HIM OFF!
SLORT
TOO BAD ABOUT THE GIANT DOG DROOL.

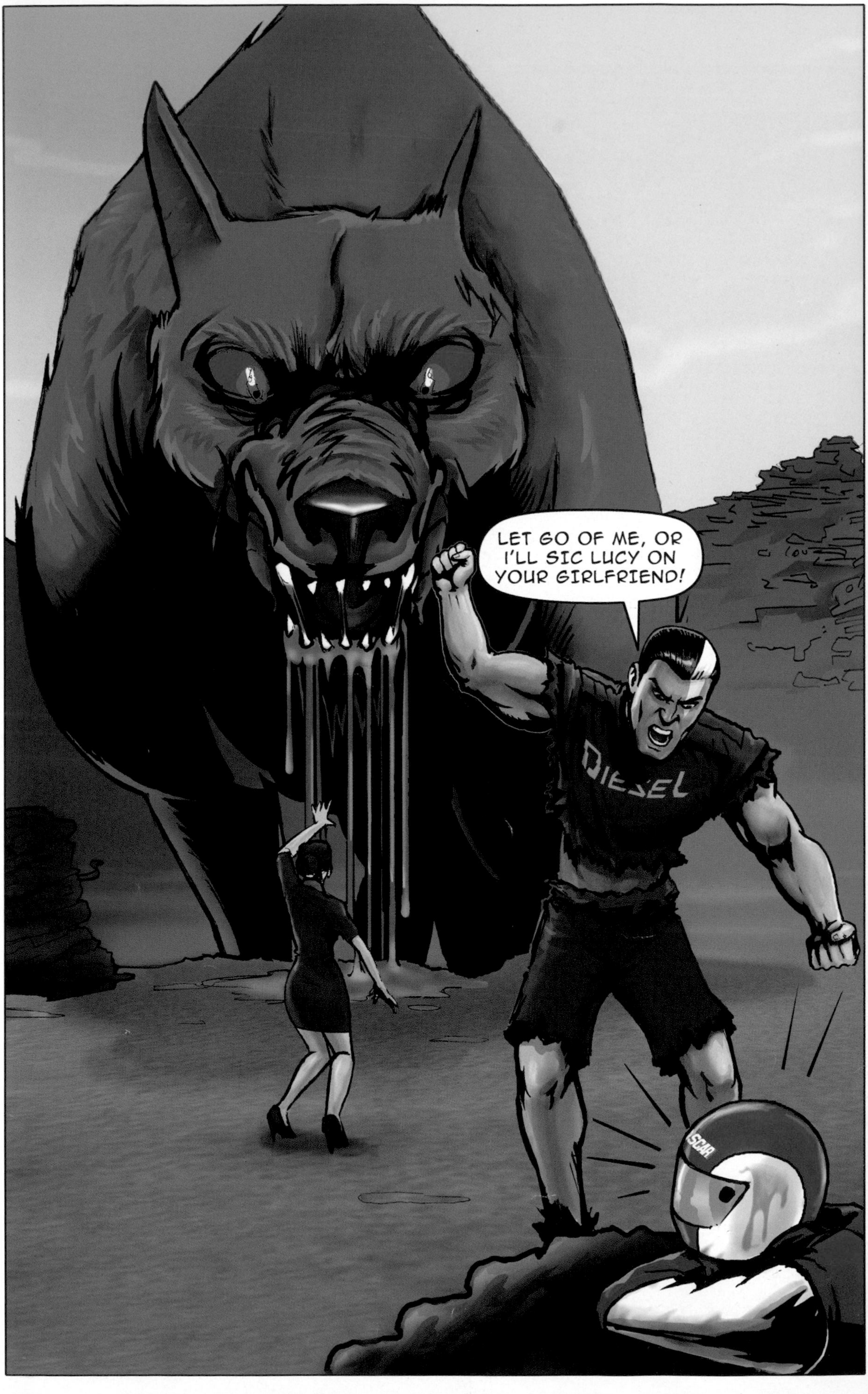
LET GO OF ME, OR I'LL SIC LUCY ON YOUR GIRLFRIEND!
DIESEL

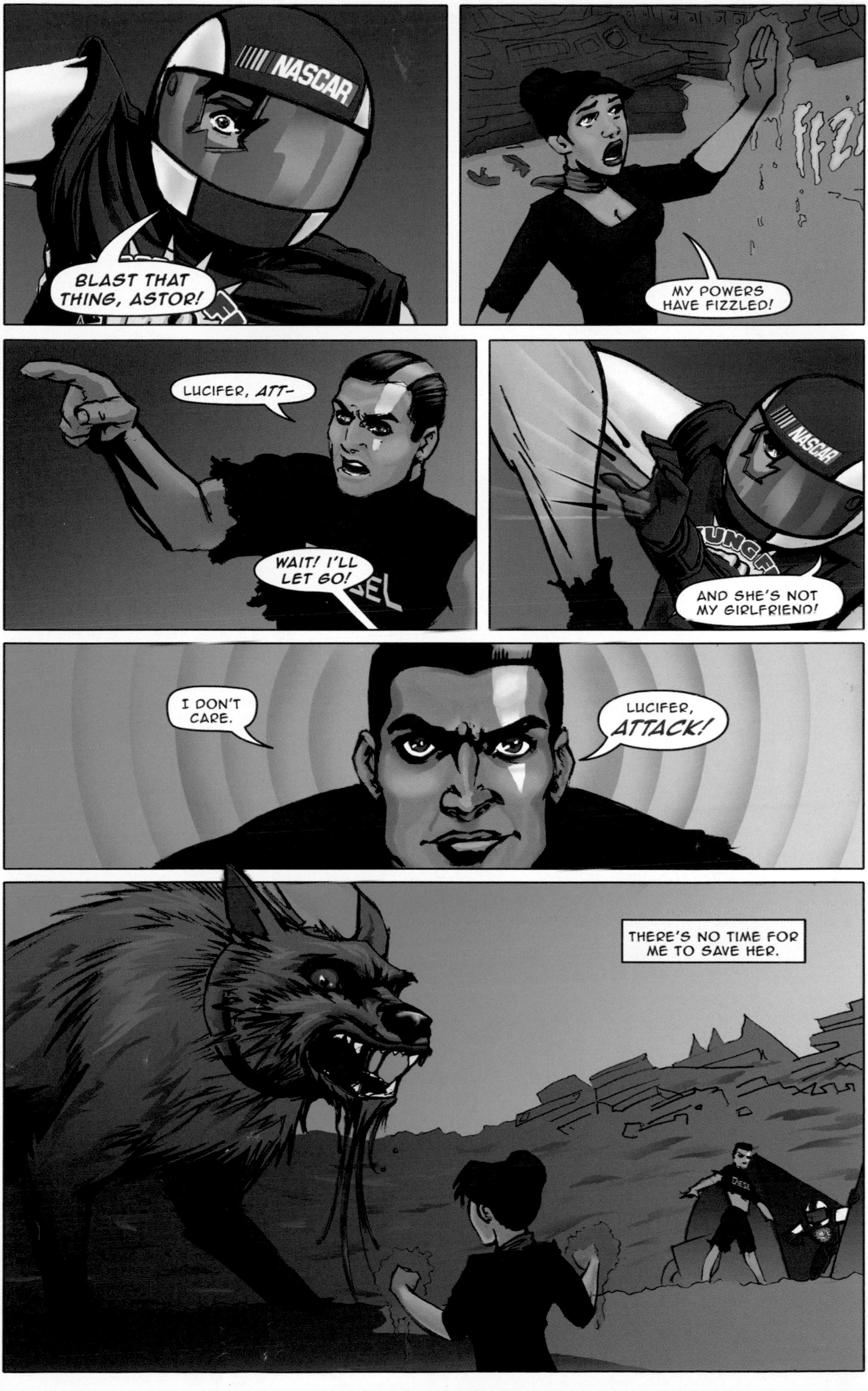
BLAST THAT THING, ASTOR!
MY POWERS HAVE FIZZLED!
LUCIFER, ATT-
WAIT! I'LL LET GO!
AND SHE'S NOT MY GIRLFRIEND!
I DON'T CARE.
LUCIFER, ATTACK!
THERE'S NO TIME FOR ME TO SAVE HER.

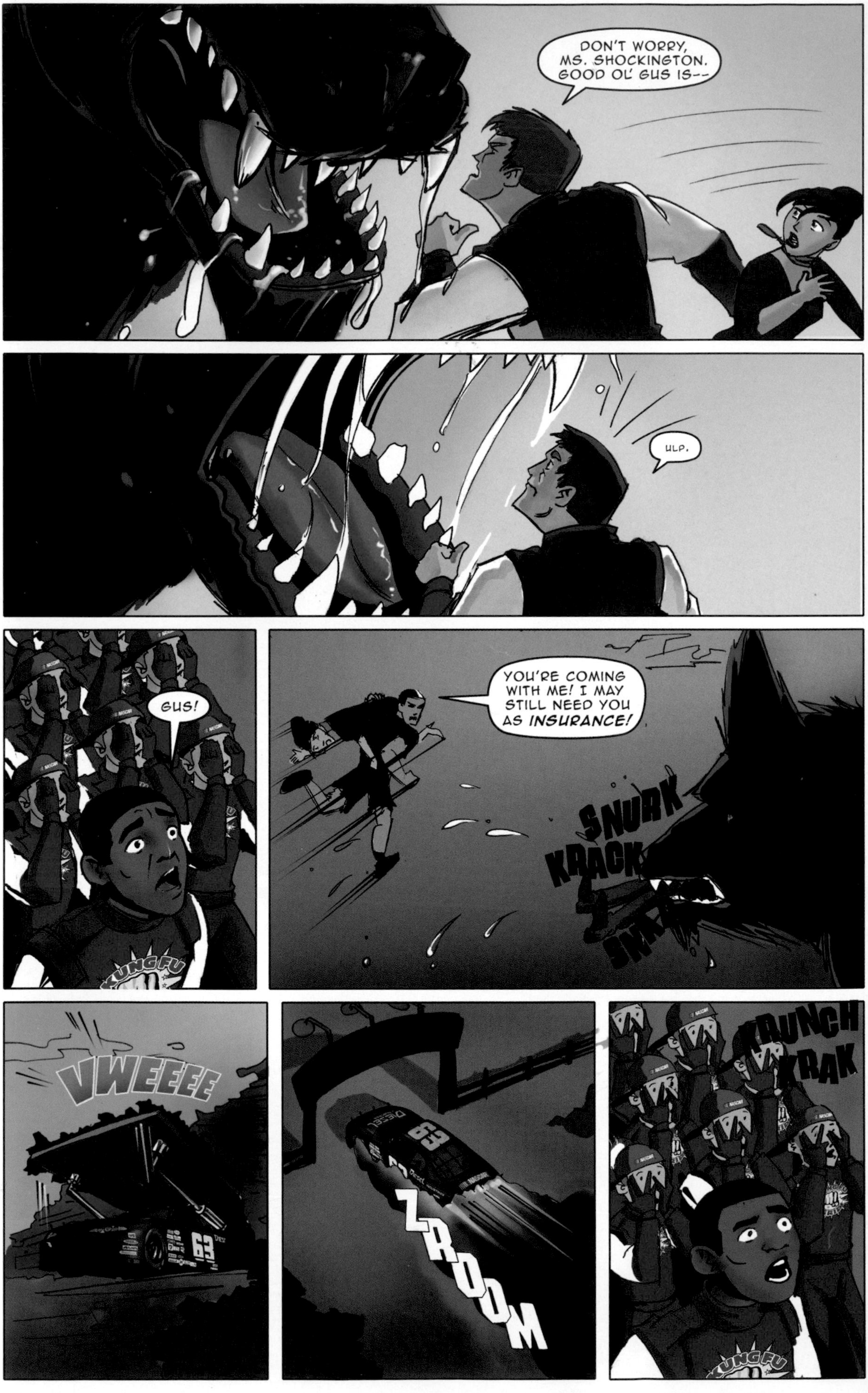
DON'T WORRY, MS. SHOCKINGTON. GOOD OL' GUS IS--
ULP.
GUS!
YOU'RE COMING WITH ME! I MAY STILL NEED YOU AS INSURANCE!
SNURK
KRACK
VWEEEE
ZROOM
KRUNCH
KRAK

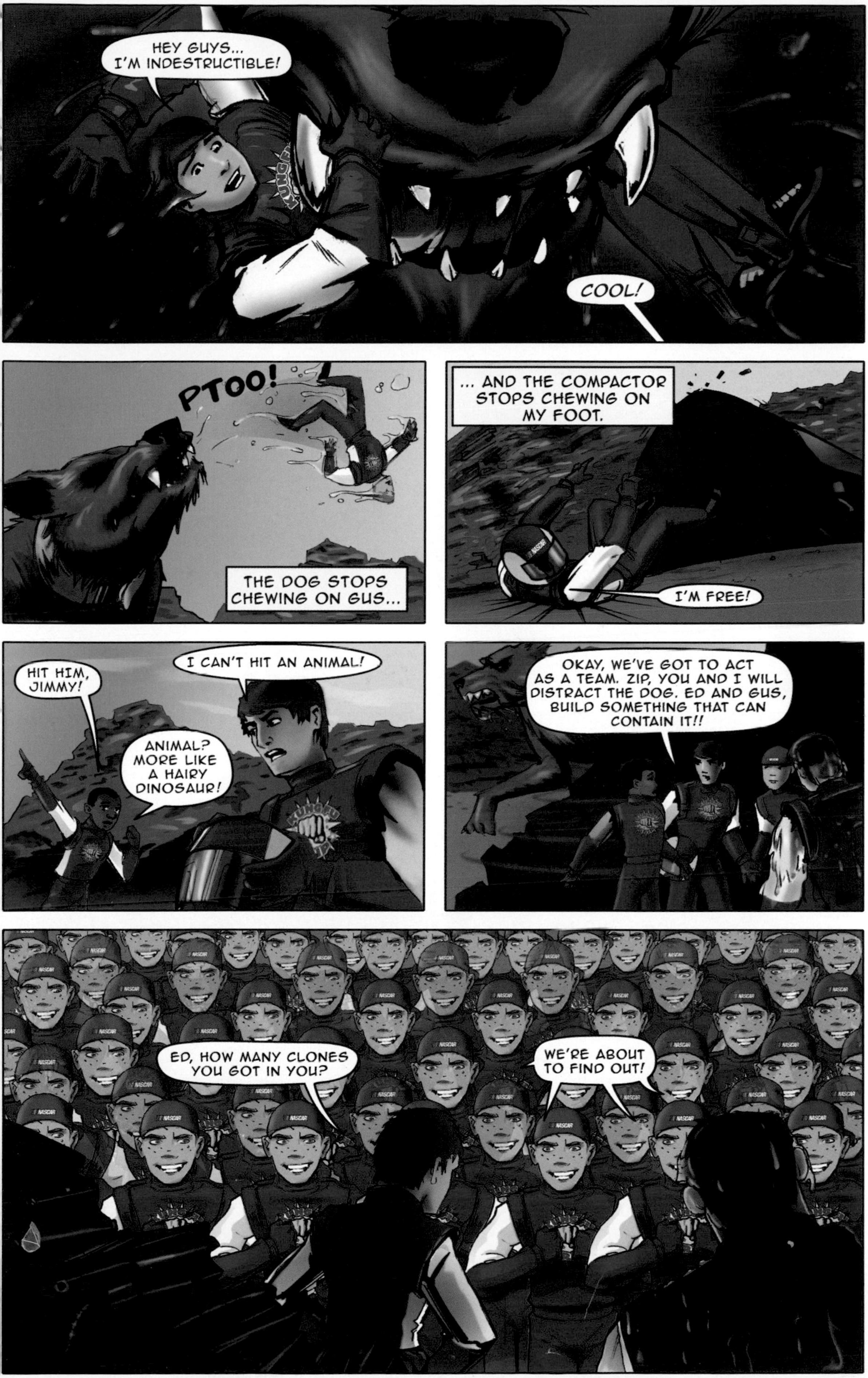
HEY GUYS... I'M INDESTRUCTIBLE!
COOL!
PTOO!
THE DOG STOPS CHEWING ON GUS...
... AND THE COMPACTOR STOPS CHEWING ON MY FOOT.
I'M FREE!
HIT HIM, JIMMY!
I CAN'T HIT AN ANIMAL!
ANIMAL? MORE LIKE A HAIRY DINOSAUR!
OKAY, WE'VE GOT TO ACT AS A TEAM. ZIP, YOU AND I WILL DISTRACT THE DOG. ED AND GUS, BUILD SOMETHING THAT CAN CONTAIN IT!!
ED, HOW MANY CLONES YOU GOT IN YOU?
WE'RE ABOUT TO FIND OUT!

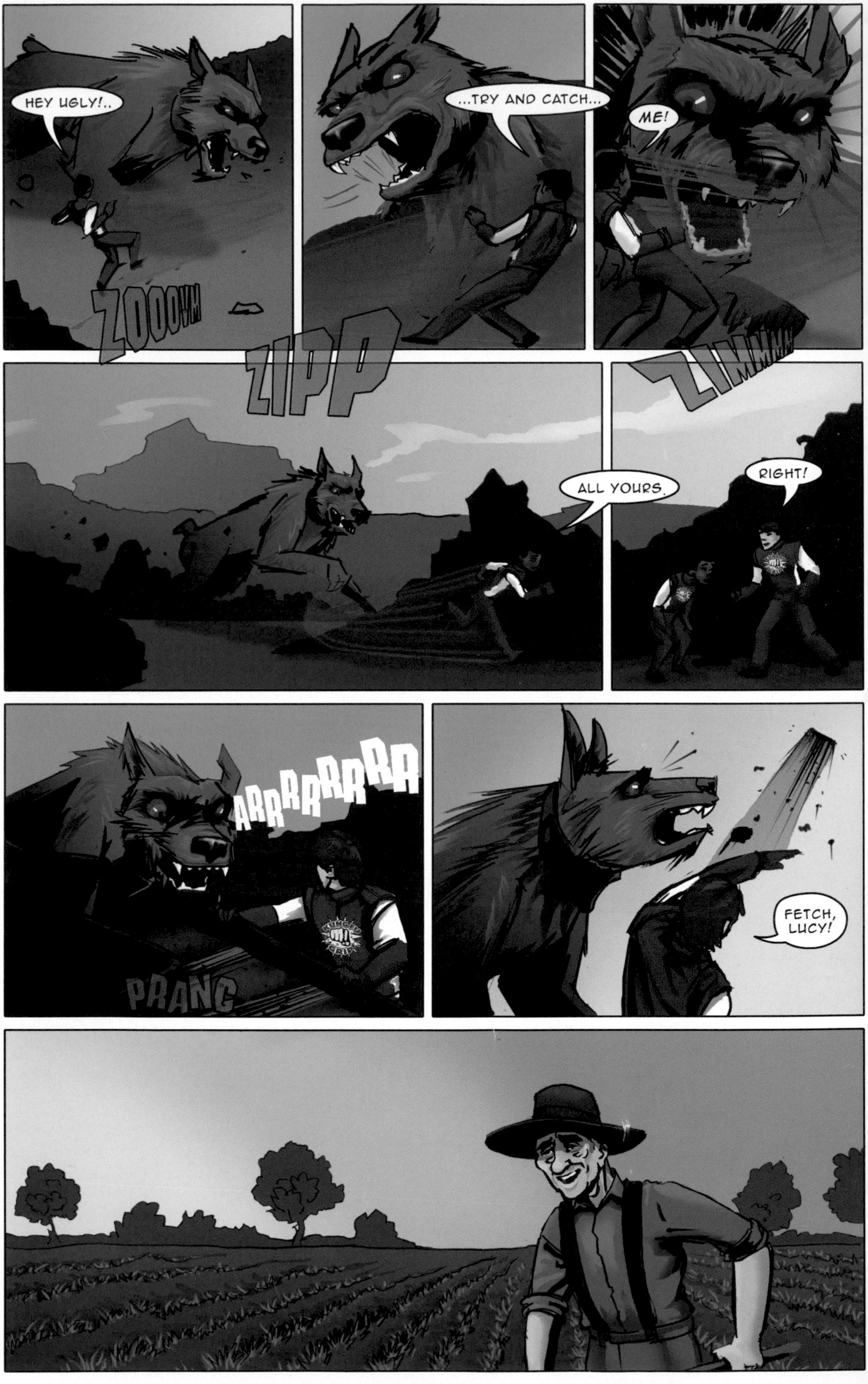
HEY UGLY!..
ZOOOVM
...TRY AND CATCH...
ME!
ZIPP
ALL YOURS.
ZIMMM
RIGHT!
ARRRRRRRA
PRANG
FETCH, LUCY!

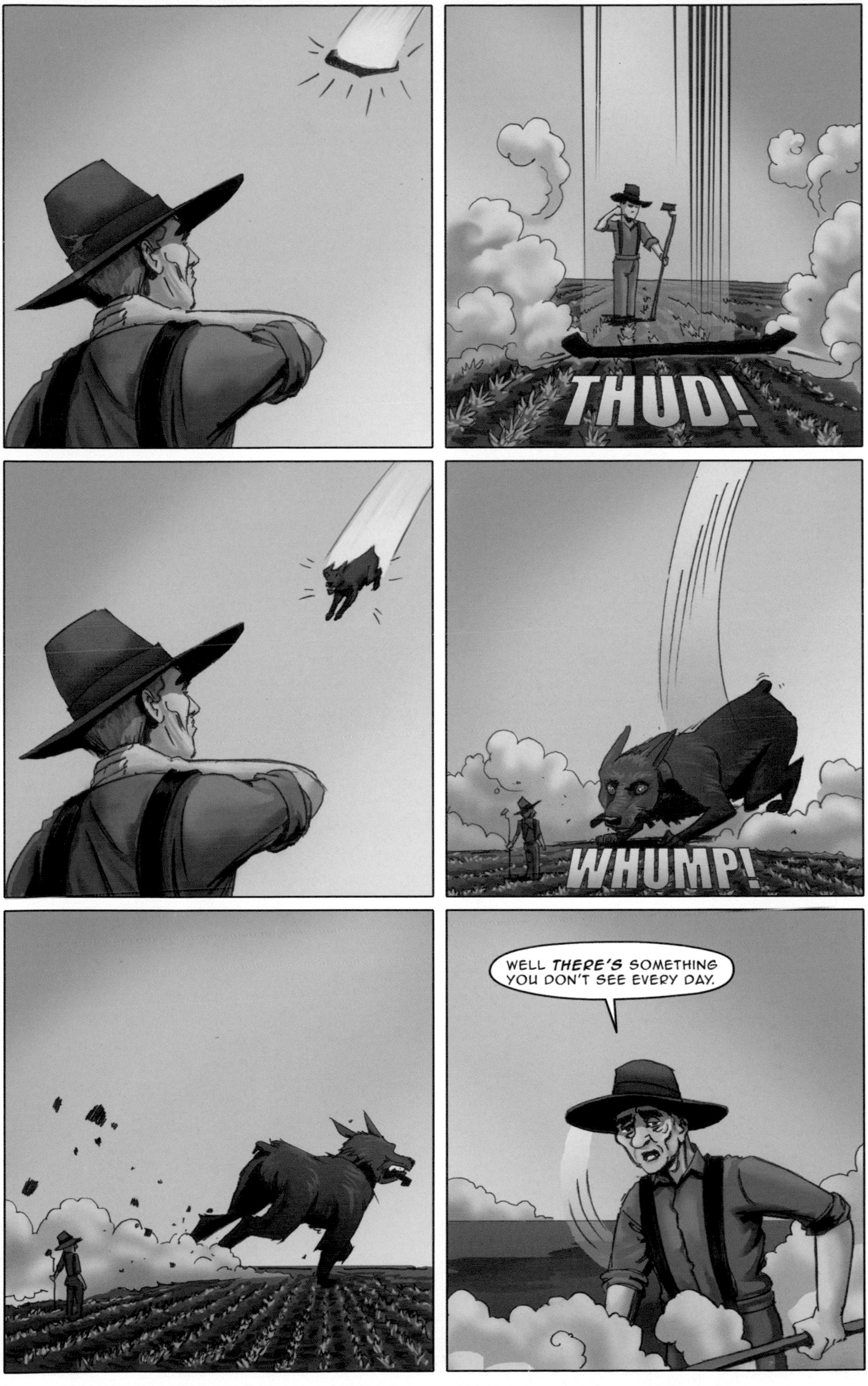
THUD!
WHUMP!
WELL *THERE'S* SOMETHING YOU DON'T SEE EVERY DAY.

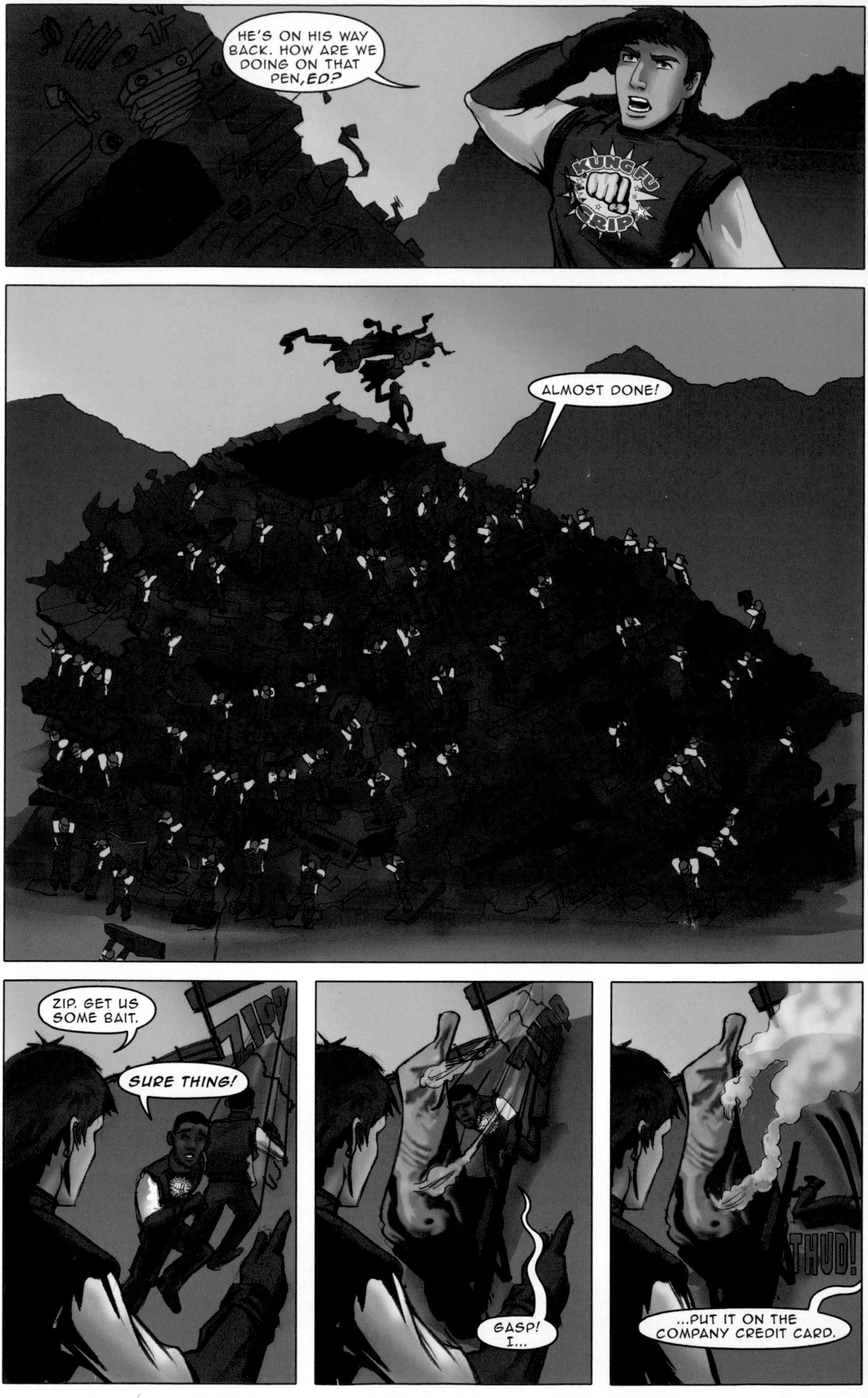
HE'S ON HIS WAY BACK. HOW ARE WE DOING ON THAT PEN, ED?
ALMOST DONE!
ZIP. GET US SOME BAIT.
SURE THING!
GASP! I...
THUD!
...PUT IT ON THE COMPANY CREDIT CARD.

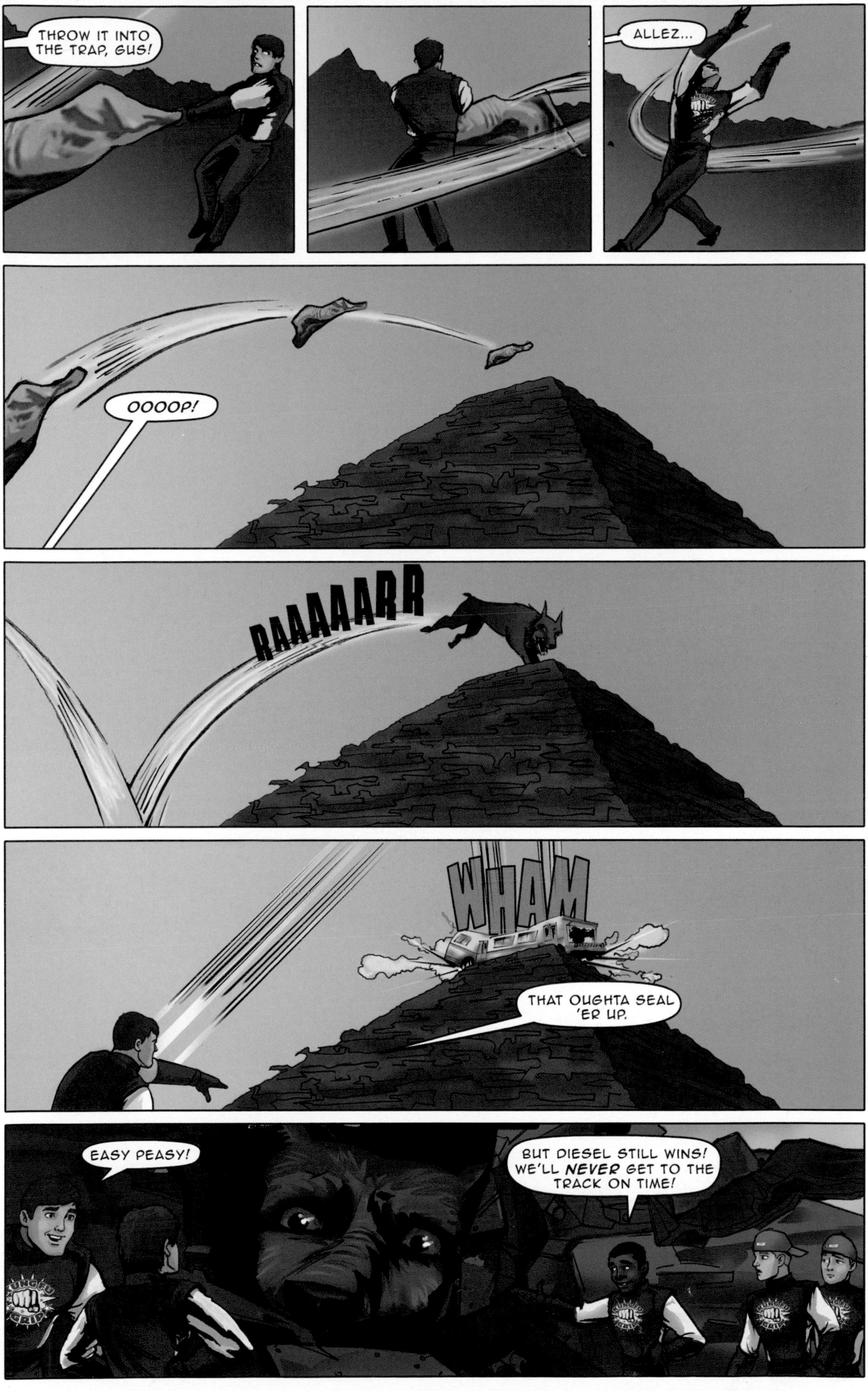
THROW IT INTO THE TRAP, GUS!
ALLEZ...
OOOOP!
RAAAAARR
WHAM
THAT OUGHTA SEAL 'ER UP.
EASY PEASY!
BUT DIESEL STILL WINS! WE'LL *NEVER* GET TO THE TRACK ON TIME!

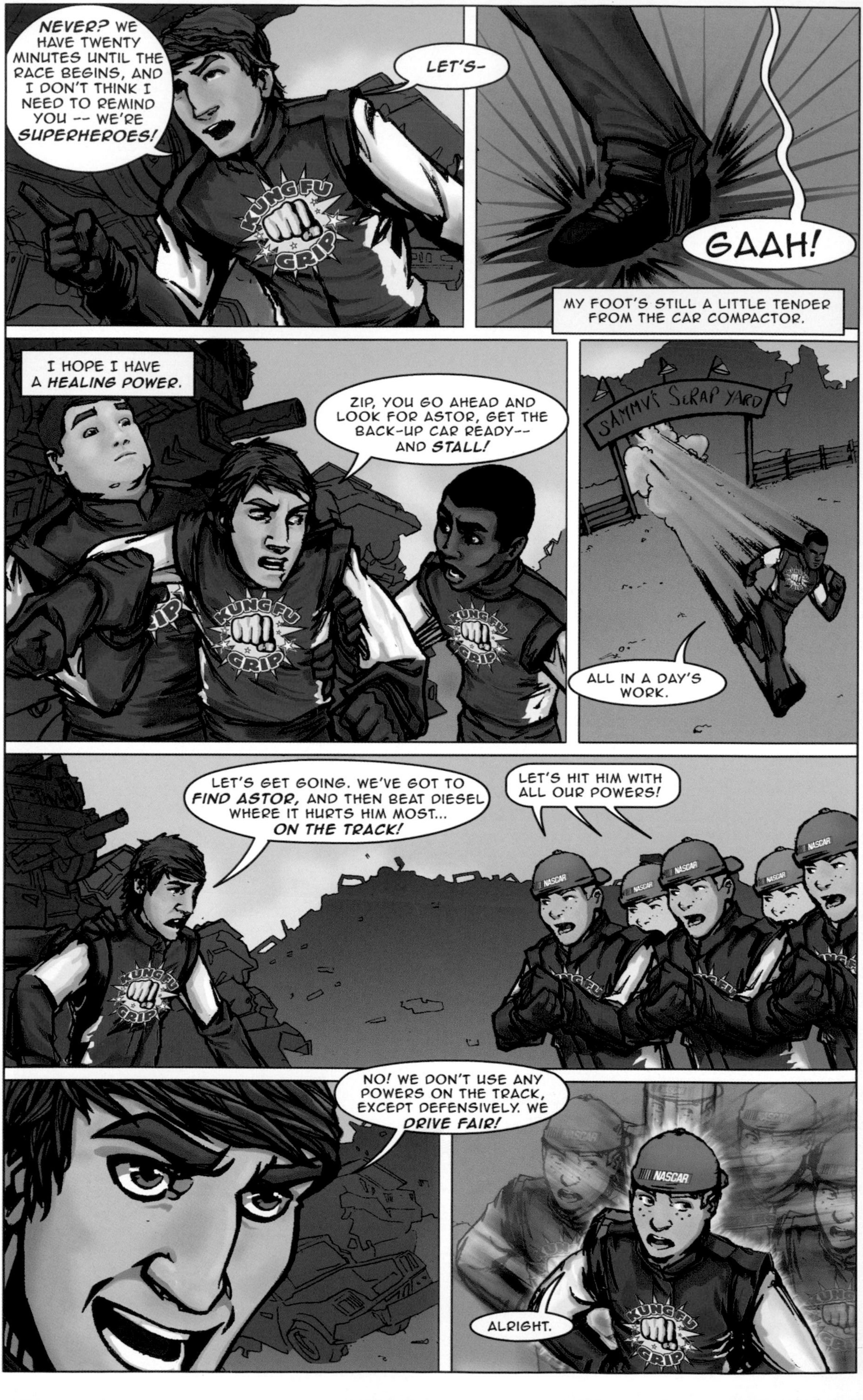
NEVER? WE HAVE TWENTY MINUTES UNTIL THE RACE BEGINS, AND I DON'T THINK I NEED TO REMIND YOU -- WE'RE SUPERHEROES!
LET'S-
GAAH!
MY FOOT'S STILL A LITTLE TENDER FROM THE CAR COMPACTOR.
I HOPE I HAVE A HEALING POWER.
ZIP, YOU GO AHEAD AND LOOK FOR ASTOR, GET THE BACK-UP CAR READY-- AND STALL!
SAMMY'S SCRAP YARD
ALL IN A DAY'S WORK.
LET'S GET GOING. WE'VE GOT TO FIND ASTOR, AND THEN BEAT DIESEL WHERE IT HURTS HIM MOST... ON THE TRACK!
LET'S HIT HIM WITH ALL OUR POWERS!
NO! WE DON'T USE ANY POWERS ON THE TRACK, EXCEPT DEFENSIVELY. WE DRIVE FAIR!
ALRIGHT.

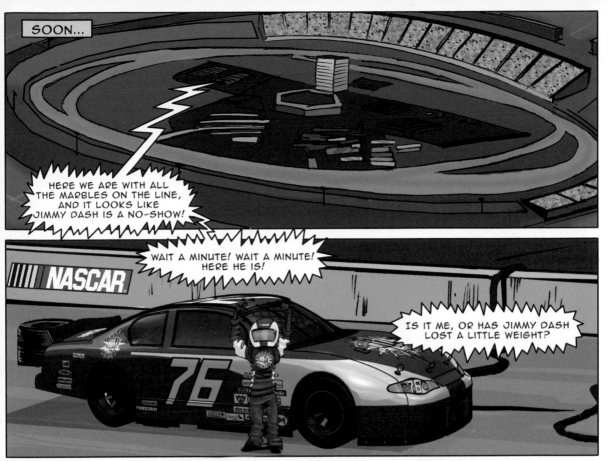

SOON...

HERE WE ARE WITH ALL THE MARBLES ON THE LINE, AND IT LOOKS LIKE JIMMY DASH IS A NO-SHOW!

WAIT A MINUTE! WAIT A MINUTE! HERE HE IS!

IS IT ME, OR HAS JIMMY DASH LOST A LITTLE WEIGHT?

OKAY, ZIP WE'RE BACK! I'LL ZIP IN, YOU ZIP OUT.

ZIP!

THANK YOU! THANK YOU!

ARE YOU LISTENING?

SORRY JIMMY, I GOT CARRIED AWAY!

I GUESS IT'S TIME TO...

...SWITCH!

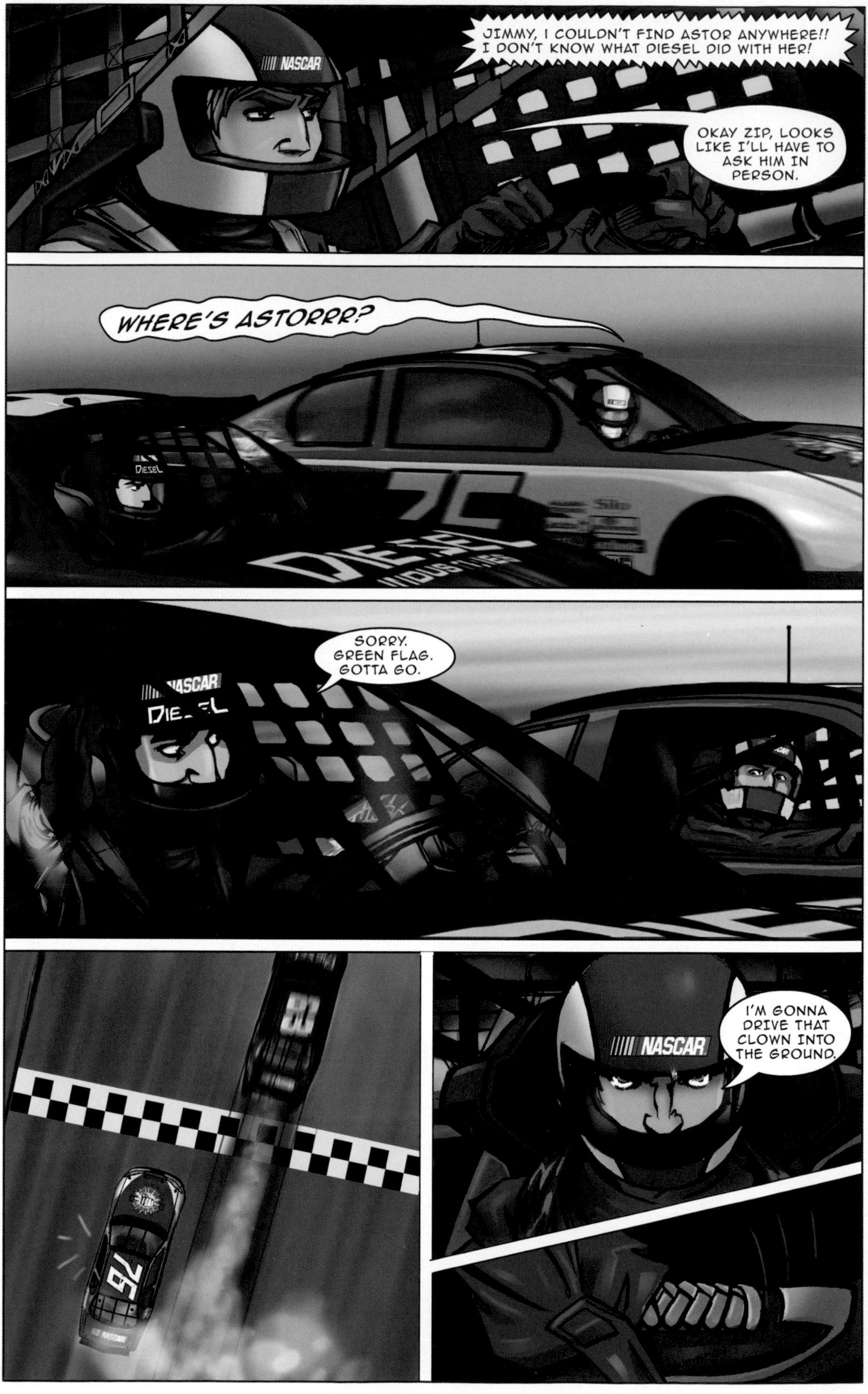
JIMMY, I COULDN'T FIND ASTOR ANYWHERE!! I DON'T KNOW WHAT DIESEL DID WITH HER!
OKAY ZIP, LOOKS LIKE I'LL HAVE TO ASK HIM IN PERSON.
NASCAR
WHERE'S ASTORRR?
DIESEL
SORRY. GREEN FLAG. GOTTA GO.
NASCAR
DIESEL
I'M GONNA DRIVE THAT CLOWN INTO THE GROUND.
NASCAR

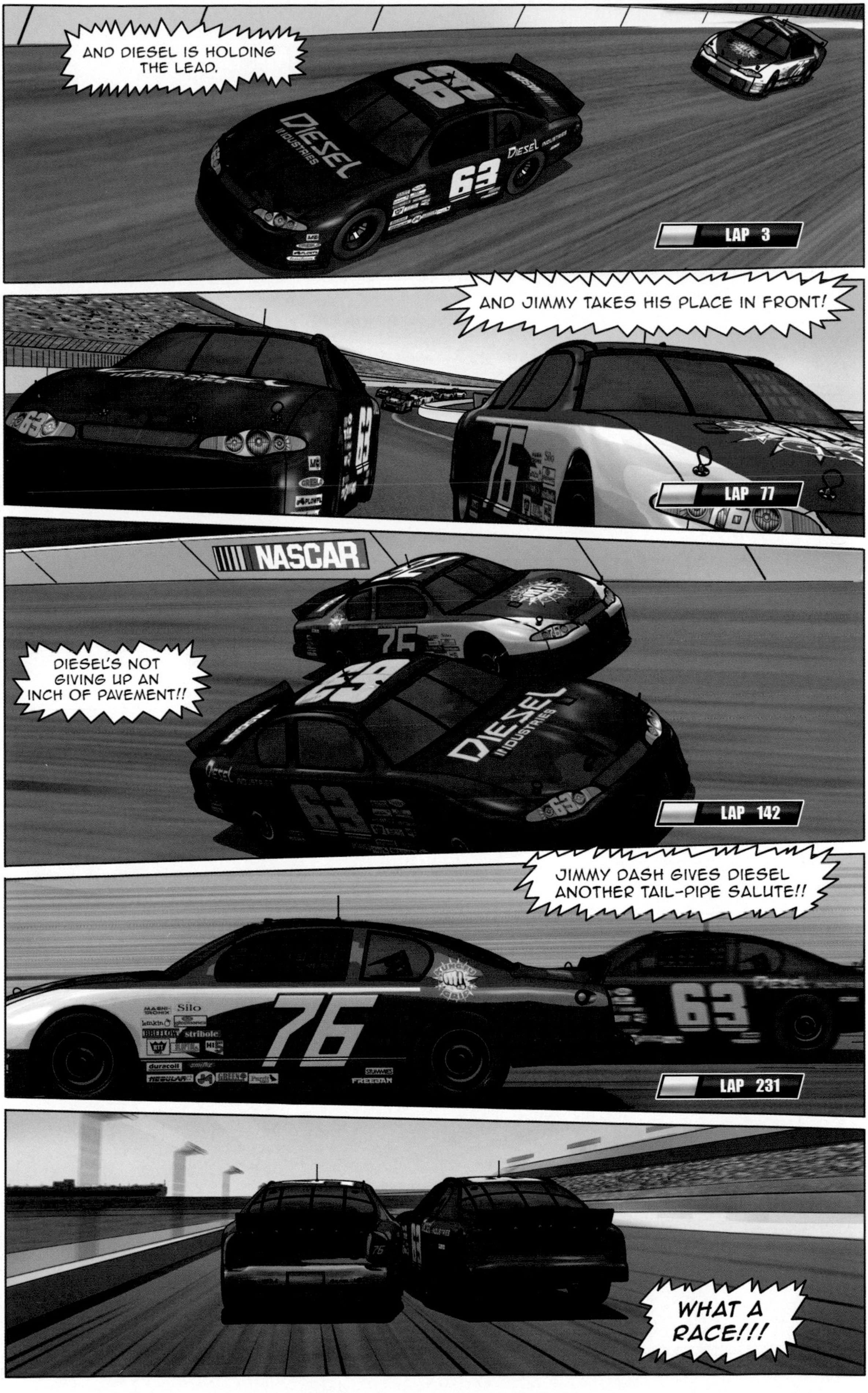
AND DIESEL IS HOLDING THE LEAD.
LAP 3
AND JIMMY TAKES HIS PLACE IN FRONT!
LAP 77
NASCAR
DIESEL'S NOT GIVING UP AN INCH OF PAVEMENT!!
LAP 142
JIMMY DASH GIVES DIESEL ANOTHER TAIL-PIPE SALUTE!!
LAP 231
WHAT A RACE!!!

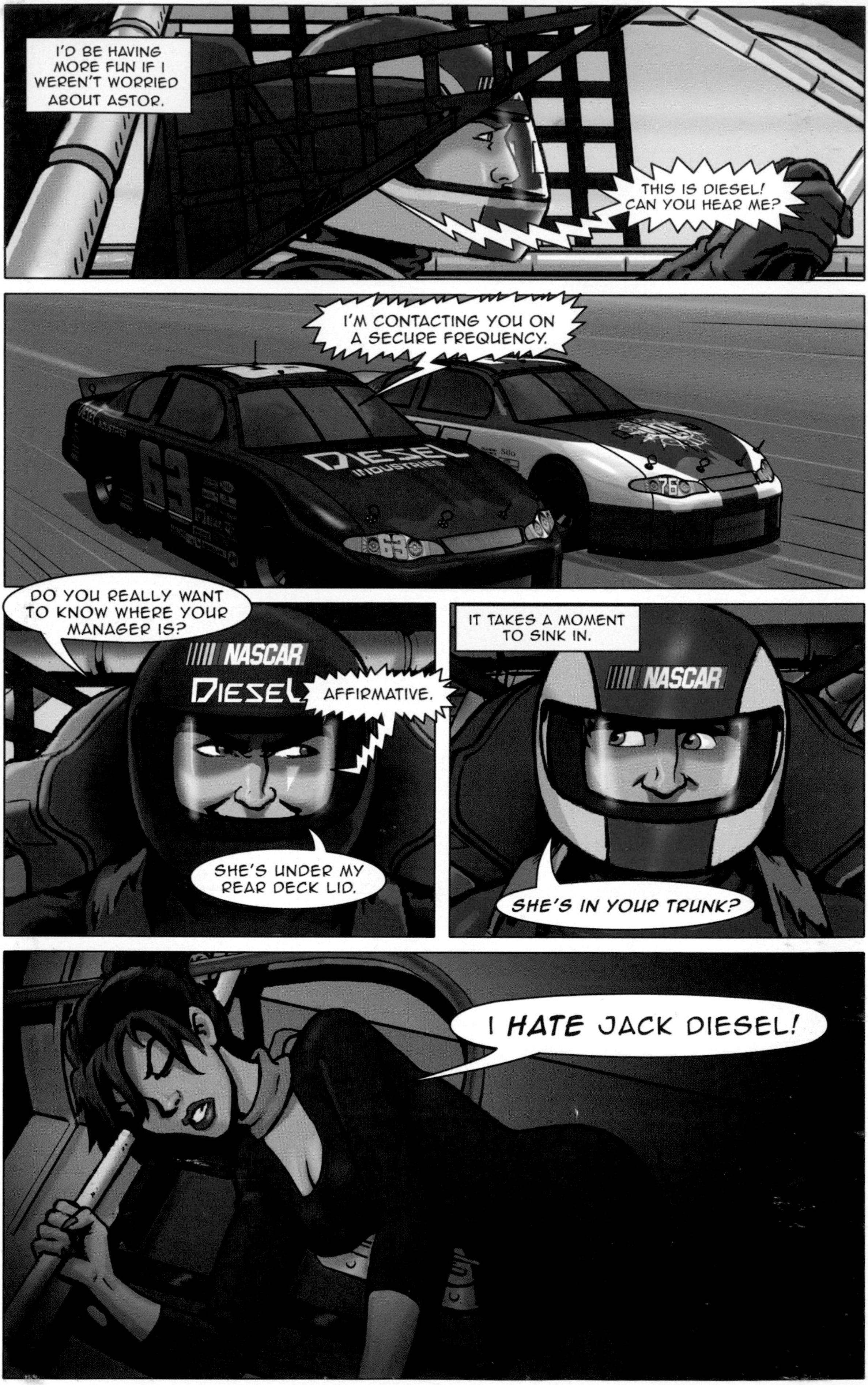
I'D BE HAVING MORE FUN IF I WEREN'T WORRIED ABOUT ASTOR.
THIS IS DIESEL! CAN YOU HEAR ME?
I'M CONTACTING YOU ON A SECURE FREQUENCY.
DIESEL INDUSTRIES
63
76
DO YOU REALLY WANT TO KNOW WHERE YOUR MANAGER IS?
NASCAR
DIESEL
AFFIRMATIVE.
SHE'S UNDER MY REAR DECK LID.
IT TAKES A MOMENT TO SINK IN.
NASCAR
SHE'S IN YOUR TRUNK?
I HATE JACK DIESEL!

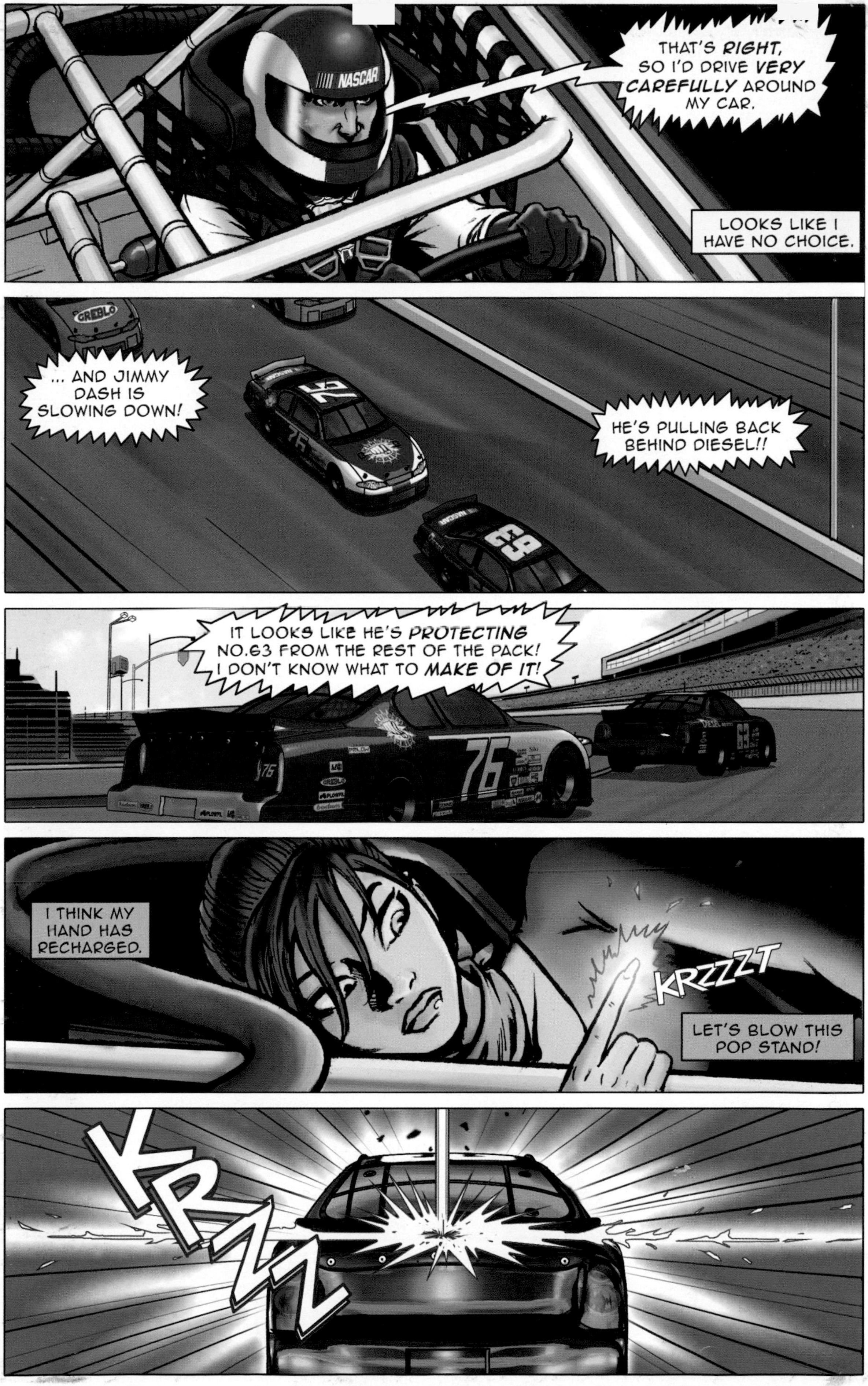
THAT'S RIGHT, SO I'D DRIVE VERY CAREFULLY AROUND MY CAR.
LOOKS LIKE I HAVE NO CHOICE.
... AND JIMMY DASH IS SLOWING DOWN!
HE'S PULLING BACK BEHIND DIESEL!!
IT LOOKS LIKE HE'S PROTECTING NO.63 FROM THE REST OF THE PACK! I DON'T KNOW WHAT TO MAKE OF IT!
I THINK MY HAND HAS RECHARGED.
KRZZZT
LET'S BLOW THIS POP STAND!
KRZZZ

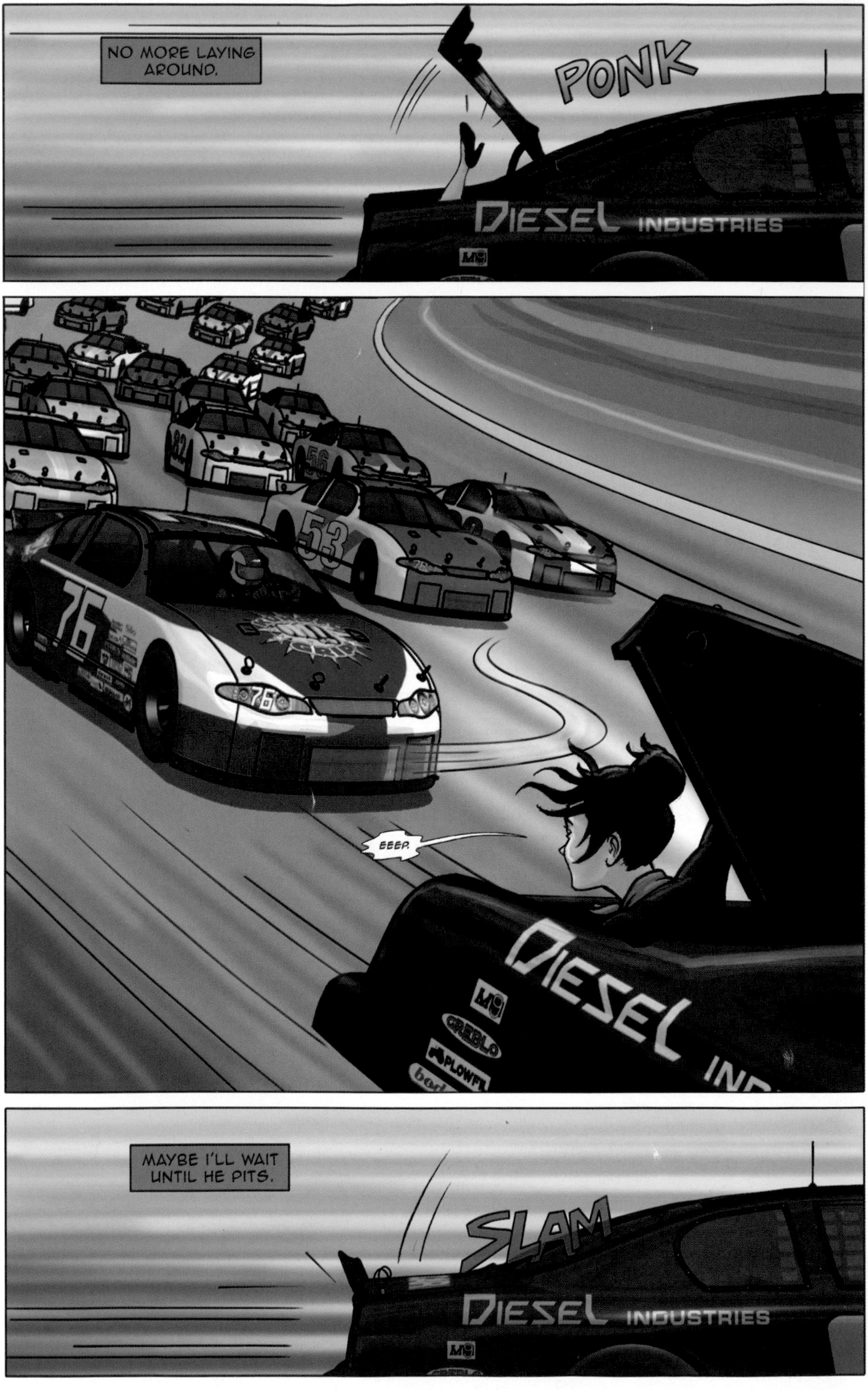
NO MORE LAYING AROUND.
PONK
DIESEL INDUSTRIES
BEEP.
DIESEL
MAYBE I'LL WAIT UNTIL HE PITS.
SLAM
DIESEL INDUSTRIES

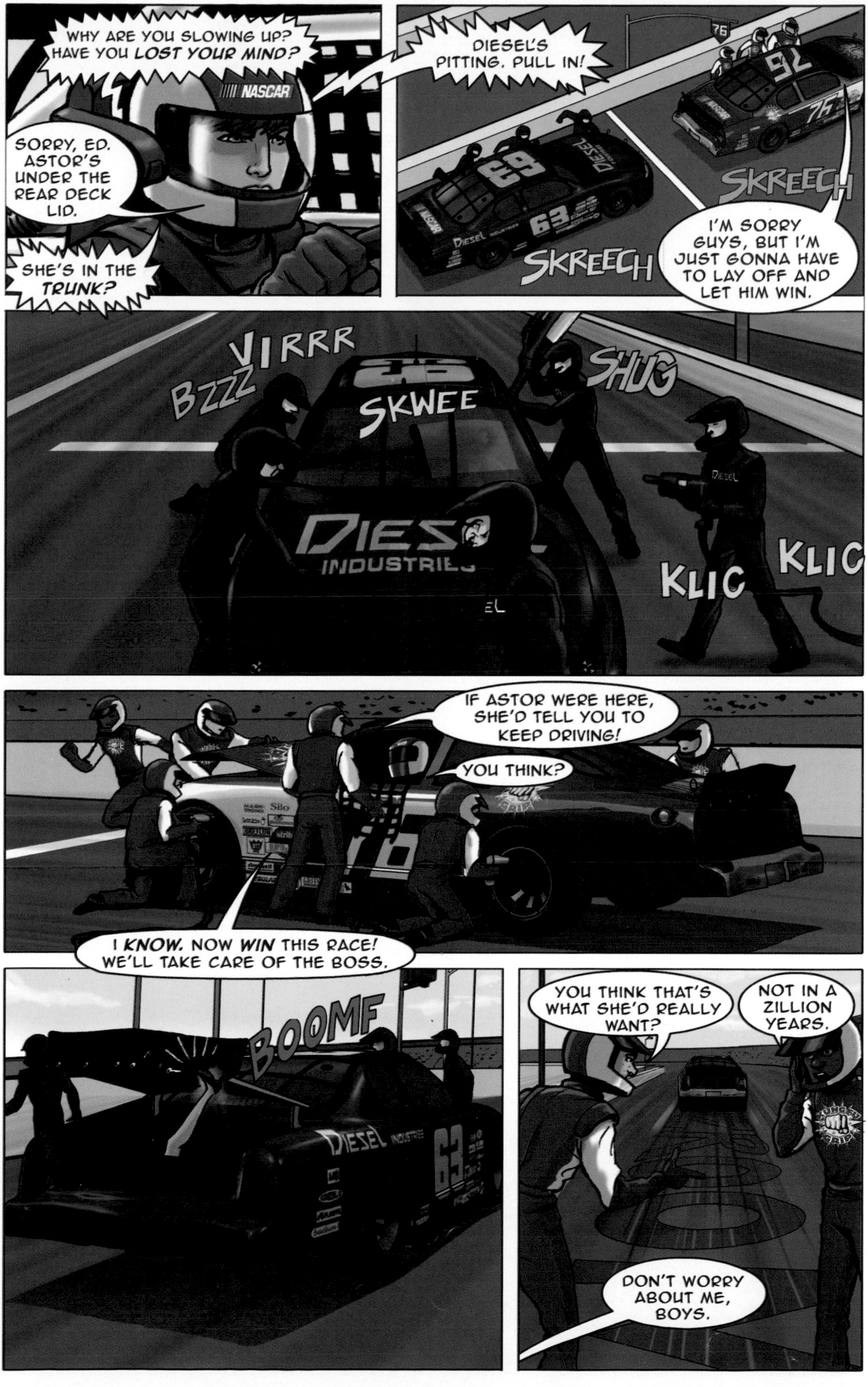
WHY ARE YOU SLOWING UP? HAVE YOU LOST YOUR MIND?
NASCAR
SORRY, ED. ASTOR'S UNDER THE REAR DECK LID.
SHE'S IN THE TRUNK?
DIESEL'S PITTING. PULL IN!
76
SKREECH
SKREECH
I'M SORRY GUYS, BUT I'M JUST GONNA HAVE TO LAY OFF AND LET HIM WIN.
VIRRR
BZZZ
SHUG
SKWEE
DIESEL
DIESEL INDUSTRIES
KLIC
KLIC
IF ASTOR WERE HERE, SHE'D TELL YOU TO KEEP DRIVING!
YOU THINK?
I KNOW. NOW WIN THIS RACE! WE'LL TAKE CARE OF THE BOSS.
BOOMF
DIESEL INDUSTRIES
63
YOU THINK THAT'S WHAT SHE'D REALLY WANT?
NOT IN A ZILLION YEARS.
DON'T WORRY ABOUT ME, BOYS.

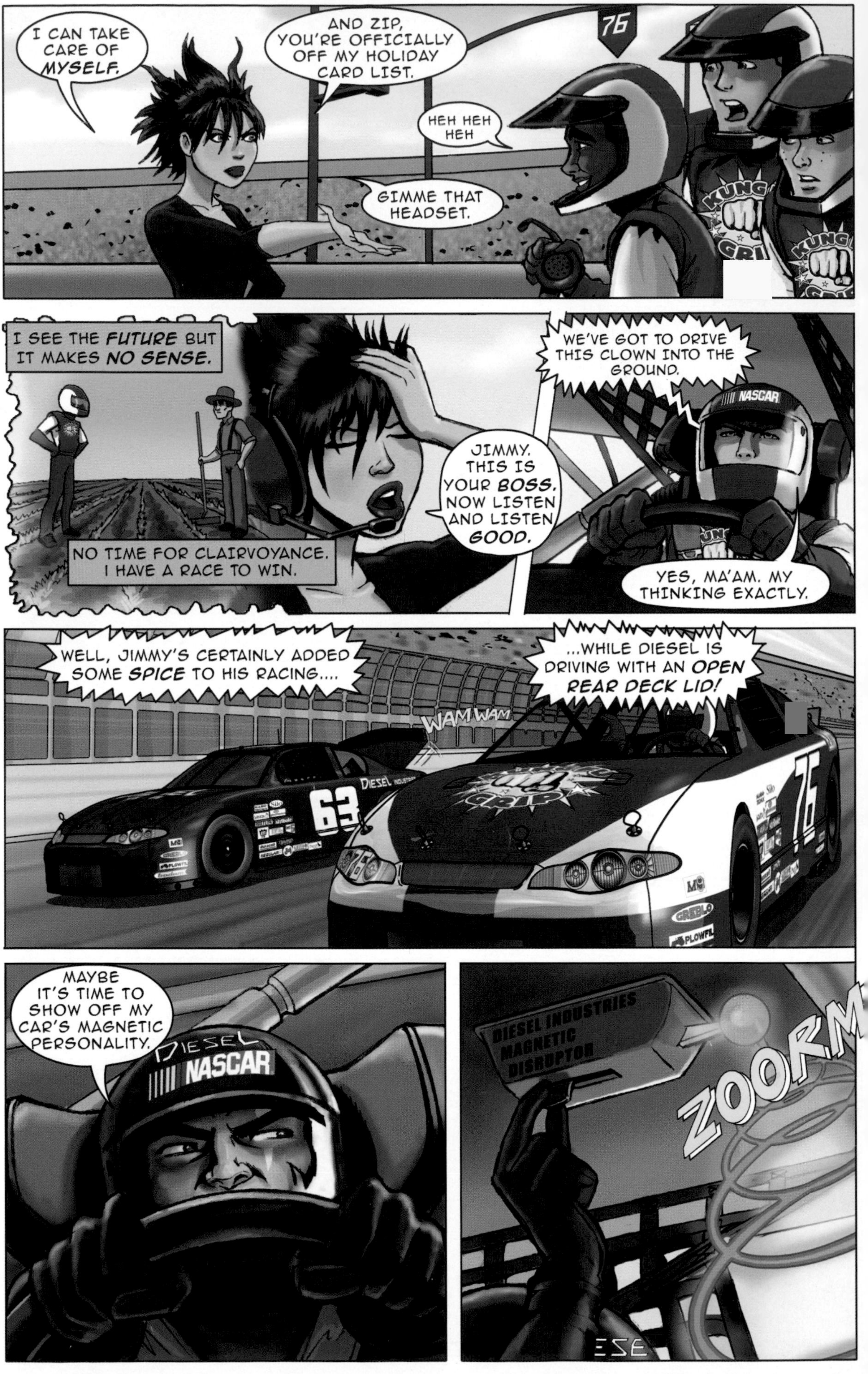
I CAN TAKE CARE OF MYSELF.
AND ZIP, YOU'RE OFFICIALLY OFF MY HOLIDAY CARD LIST.
76
HEH HEH HEH
GIMME THAT HEADSET.
KUNG GRIP
I SEE THE FUTURE BUT IT MAKES NO SENSE.
NO TIME FOR CLAIRVOYANCE. I HAVE A RACE TO WIN.
JIMMY. THIS IS YOUR BOSS. NOW LISTEN AND LISTEN GOOD.
WE'VE GOT TO DRIVE THIS CLOWN INTO THE GROUND.
NASCAR
YES, MA'AM. MY THINKING EXACTLY.
WELL, JIMMY'S CERTAINLY ADDED SOME SPICE TO HIS RACING....
...WHILE DIESEL IS DRIVING WITH AN OPEN REAR DECK LID!
WAM WAM
DIESEL INDUSTRIES
63
76
GRIP
PLOWFL
MAYBE IT'S TIME TO SHOW OFF MY CAR'S MAGNETIC PERSONALITY.
DIESEL
NASCAR
DIESEL INDUSTRIES MAGNETIC DISRUPTOR
ZOORM

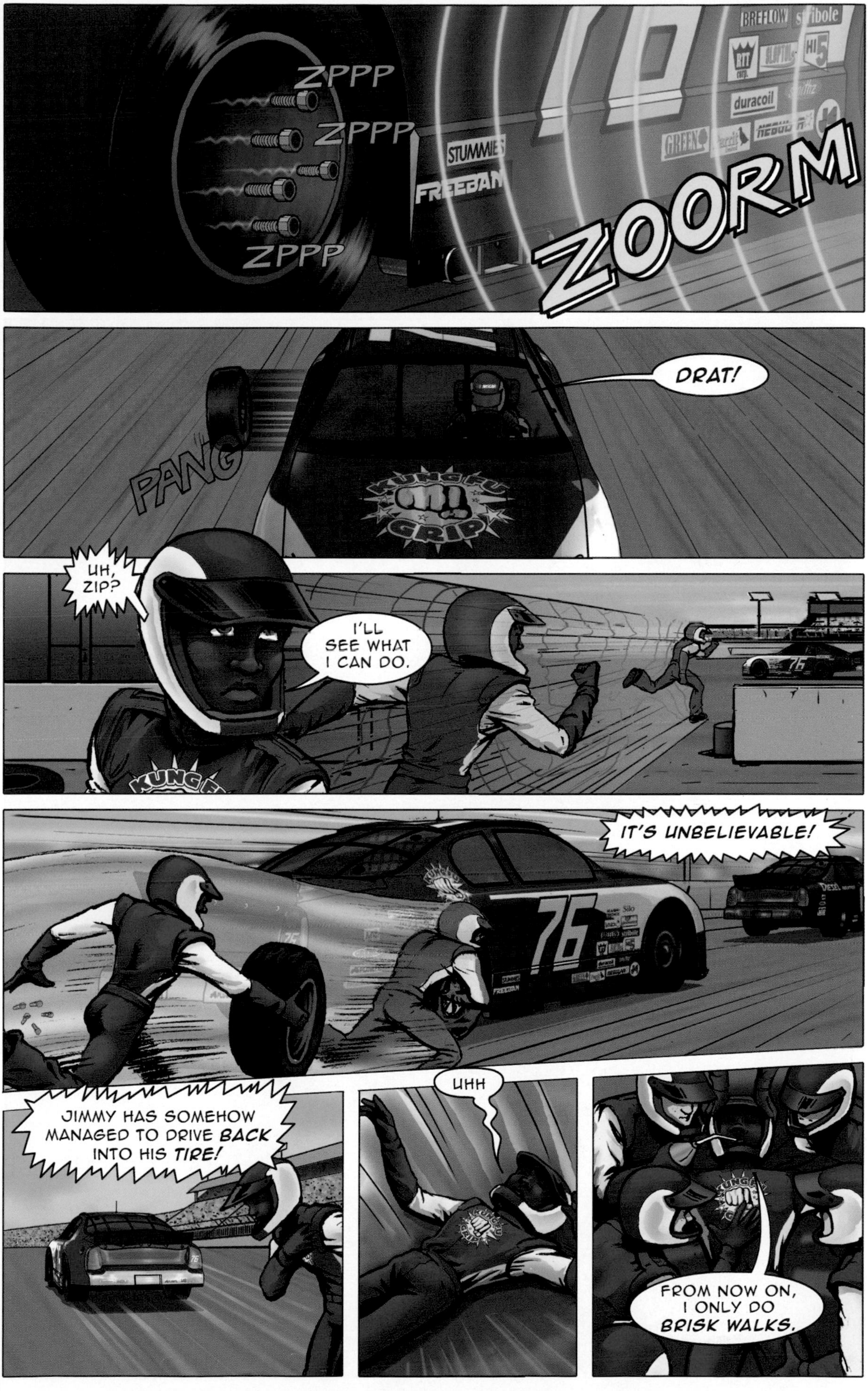

ZPPP
ZPPP
ZPPP
ZOORM
DRAT!
PANG
UH, ZIP?
I'LL SEE WHAT I CAN DO.
IT'S UNBELIEVABLE!
JIMMY HAS SOMEHOW MANAGED TO DRIVE BACK INTO HIS TIRE!
UHH
FROM NOW ON, I ONLY DO BRISK WALKS.

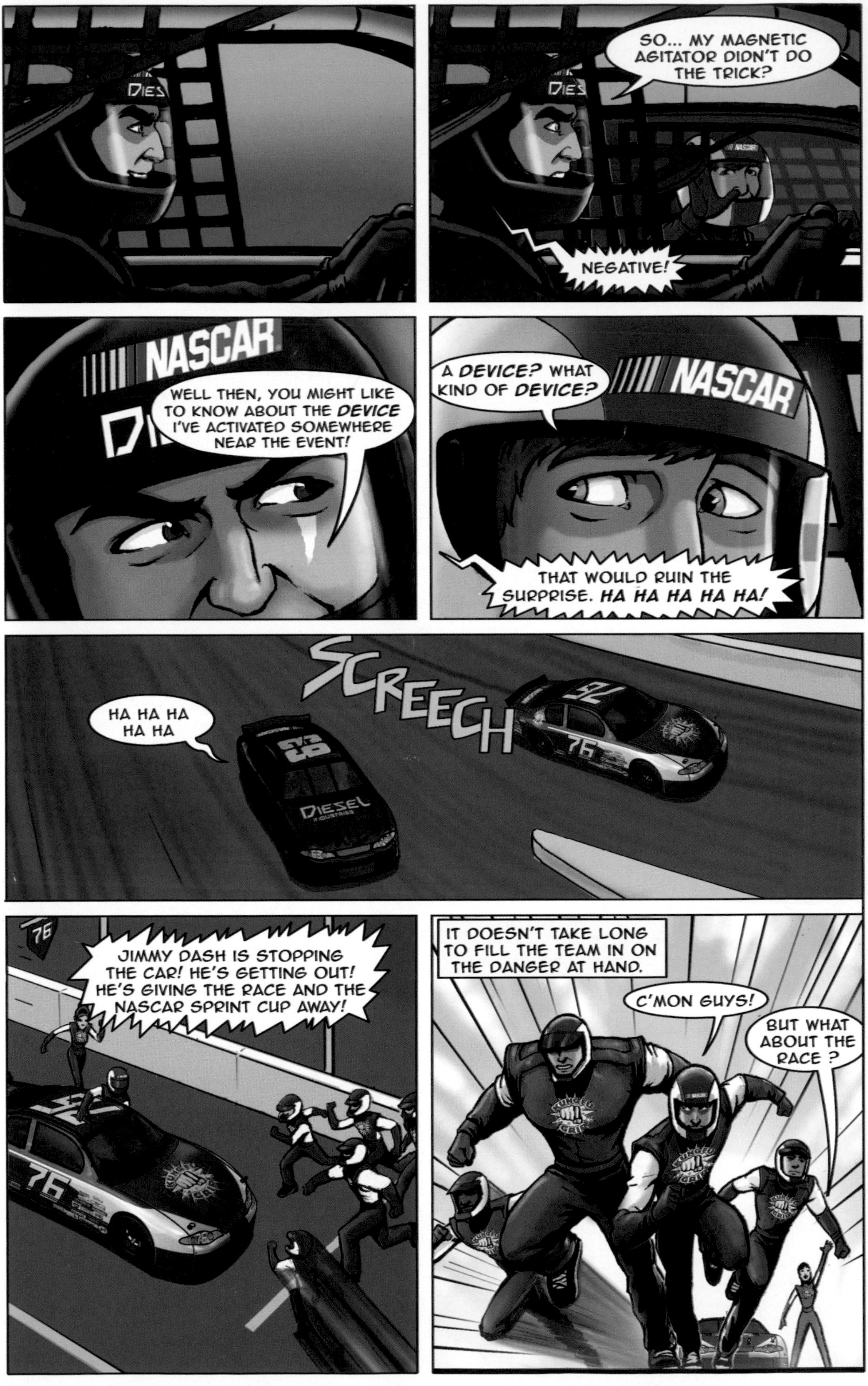
DIES
SO... MY MAGNETIC AGITATOR DIDN'T DO THE TRICK?
NEGATIVE!
NASCAR
WELL THEN, YOU MIGHT LIKE TO KNOW ABOUT THE *DEVICE* I'VE ACTIVATED SOMEWHERE NEAR THE EVENT!
A *DEVICE?* WHAT KIND OF *DEVICE?*
NASCAR
THAT WOULD RUIN THE SURPRISE. ***HA HA HA HA HA!***
SCREECH
HA HA HA HA HA
DIESEL
76
JIMMY DASH IS STOPPING THE CAR! HE'S GETTING OUT! HE'S GIVING THE RACE AND THE NASCAR SPRINT CUP AWAY!
IT DOESN'T TAKE LONG TO FILL THE TEAM IN ON THE DANGER AT HAND.
C'MON GUYS!
BUT WHAT ABOUT THE RACE ?

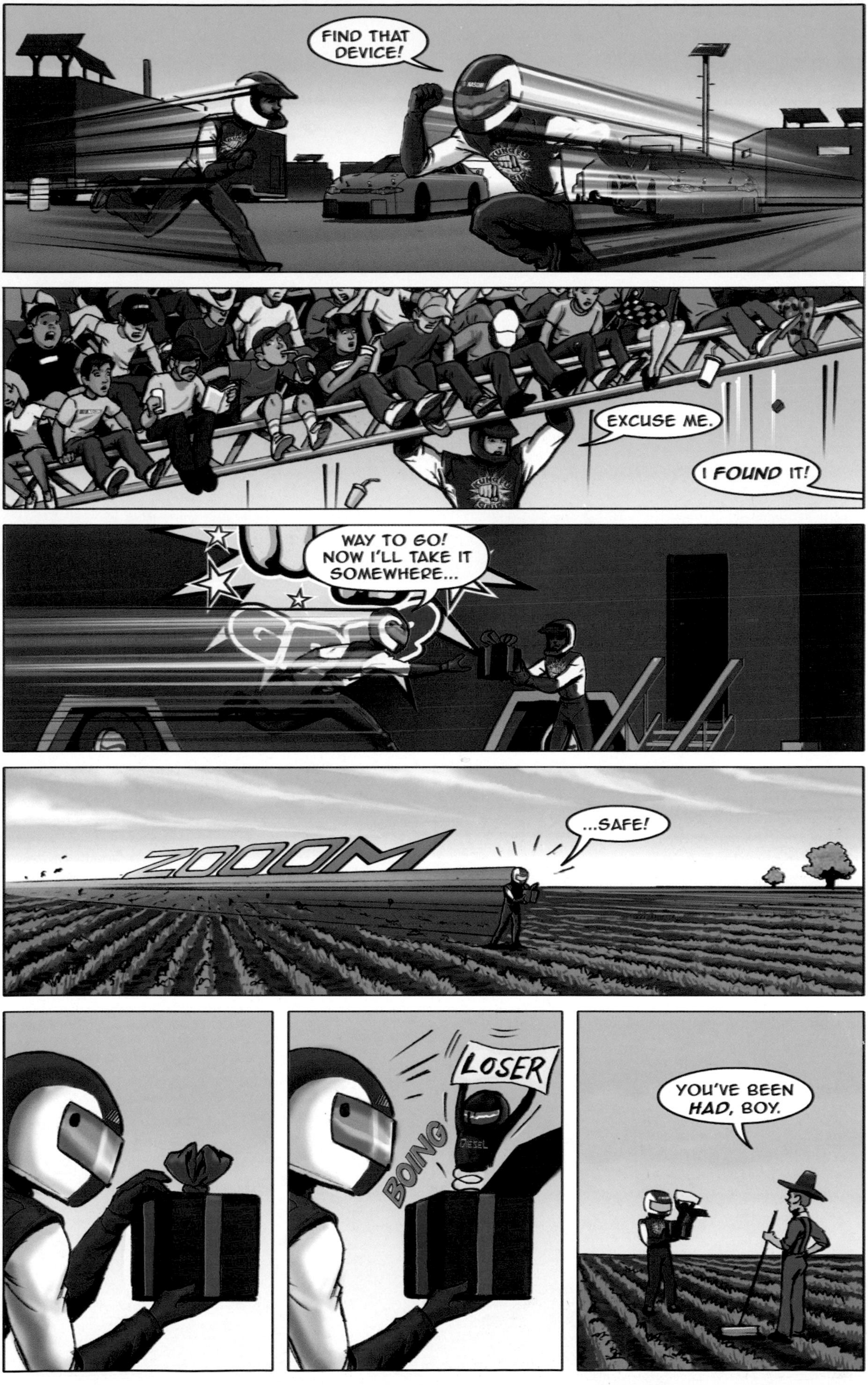

FIND THAT DEVICE!
EXCUSE ME.
I FOUND IT!
WAY TO GO! NOW I'LL TAKE IT SOMEWHERE...
ZOOOM
...SAFE!
LOSER
BOING
DIESEL
YOU'VE BEEN HAD, BOY.

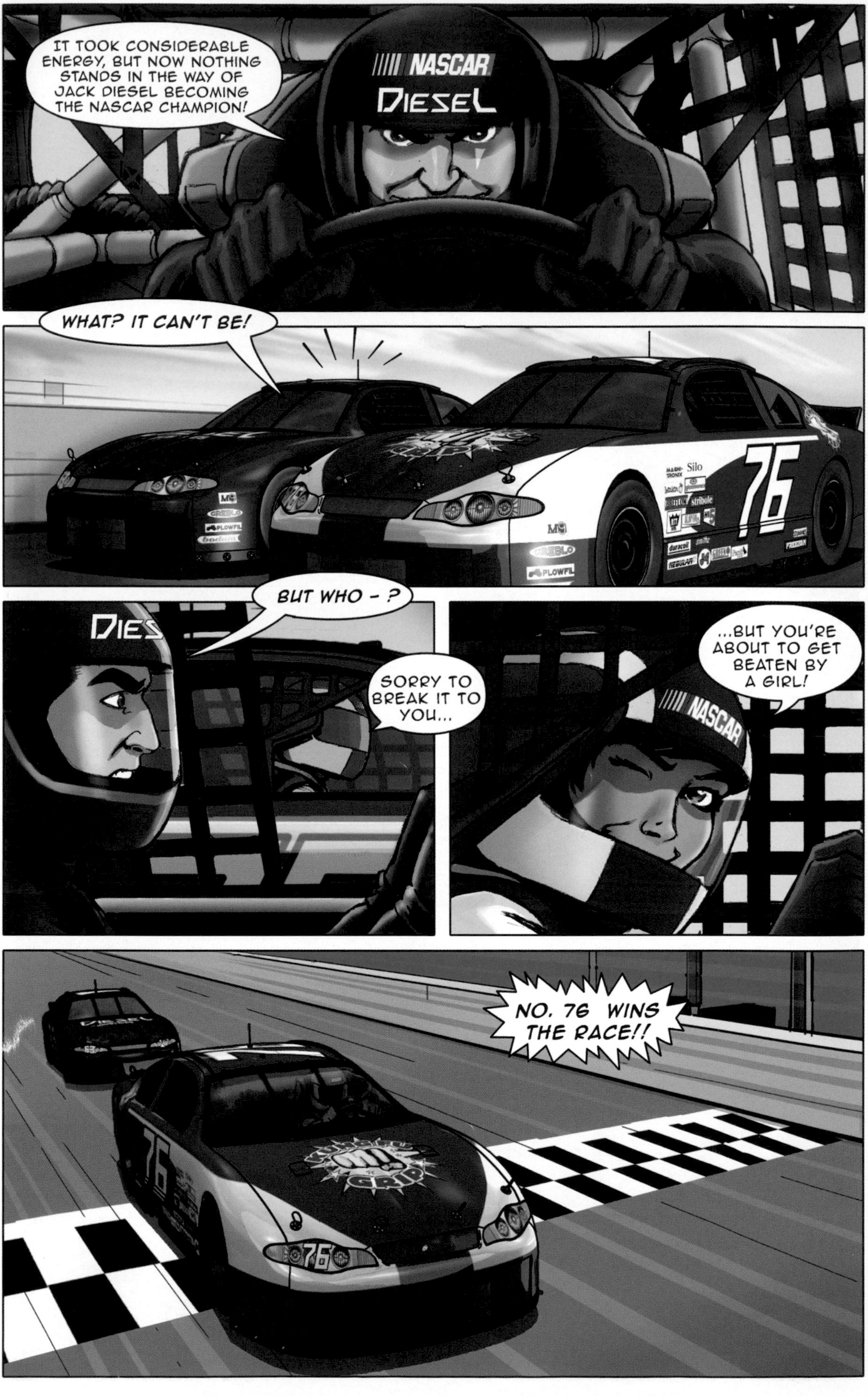
IT TOOK CONSIDERABLE ENERGY, BUT NOW NOTHING STANDS IN THE WAY OF JACK DIESEL BECOMING THE NASCAR CHAMPION!
WHAT? IT CAN'T BE!
BUT WHO - ?
SORRY TO BREAK IT TO YOU...
...BUT YOU'RE ABOUT TO GET BEATEN BY A GIRL!
NO. 76 WINS THE RACE!!

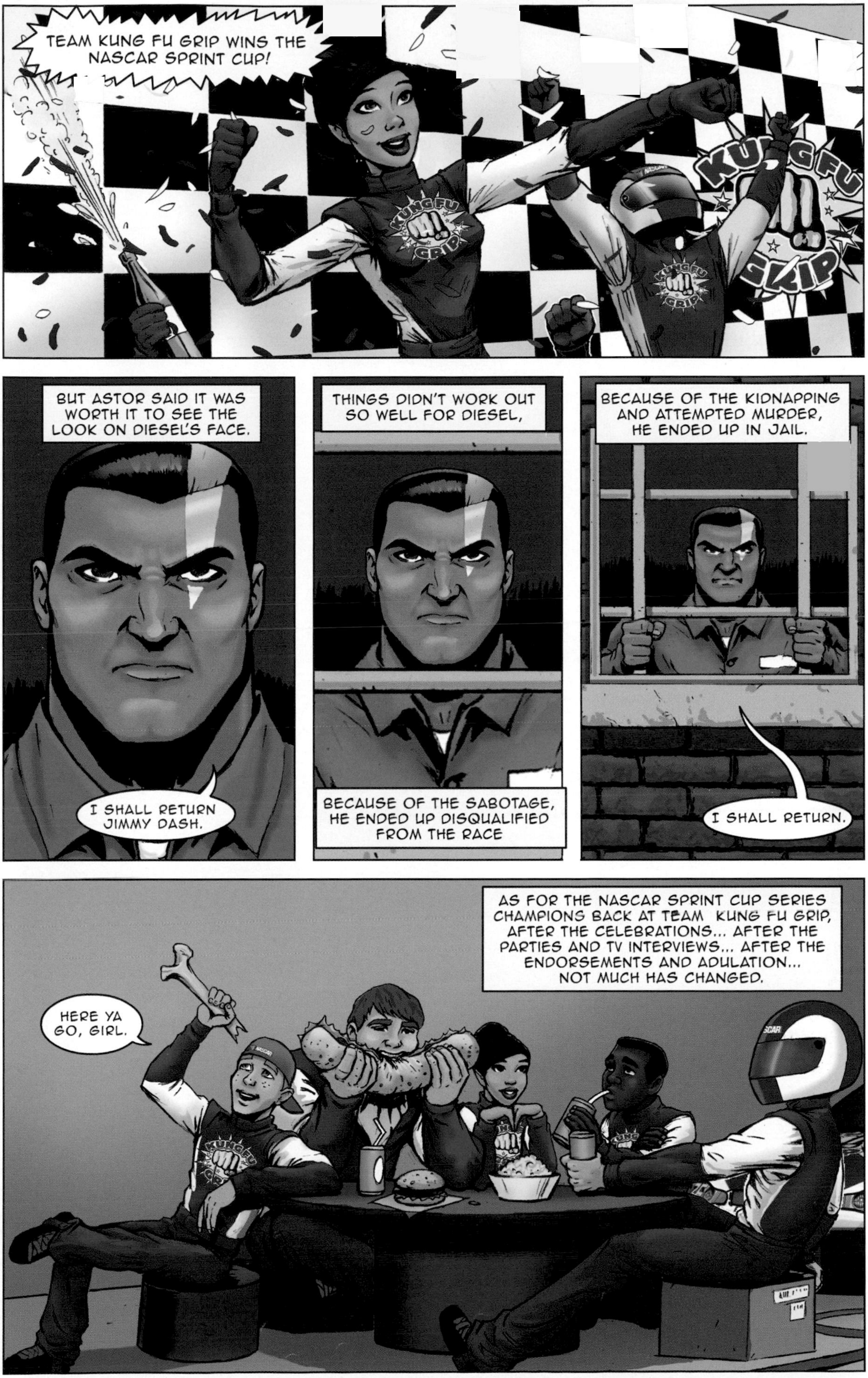
TEAM KUNG FU GRIP WINS THE NASCAR SPRINT CUP!
KUNG FU GRIP
BUT ASTOR SAID IT WAS WORTH IT TO SEE THE LOOK ON DIESEL'S FACE.
I SHALL RETURN JIMMY DASH.
THINGS DIDN'T WORK OUT SO WELL FOR DIESEL,
BECAUSE OF THE SABOTAGE, HE ENDED UP DISQUALIFIED FROM THE RACE
BECAUSE OF THE KIDNAPPING AND ATTEMPTED MURDER, HE ENDED UP IN JAIL.
I SHALL RETURN.
AS FOR THE NASCAR SPRINT CUP SERIES CHAMPIONS BACK AT TEAM KUNG FU GRIP, AFTER THE CELEBRATIONS... AFTER THE PARTIES AND TV INTERVIEWS... AFTER THE ENDORSEMENTS AND ADULATION... NOT MUCH HAS CHANGED.
HERE YA GO, GIRL.

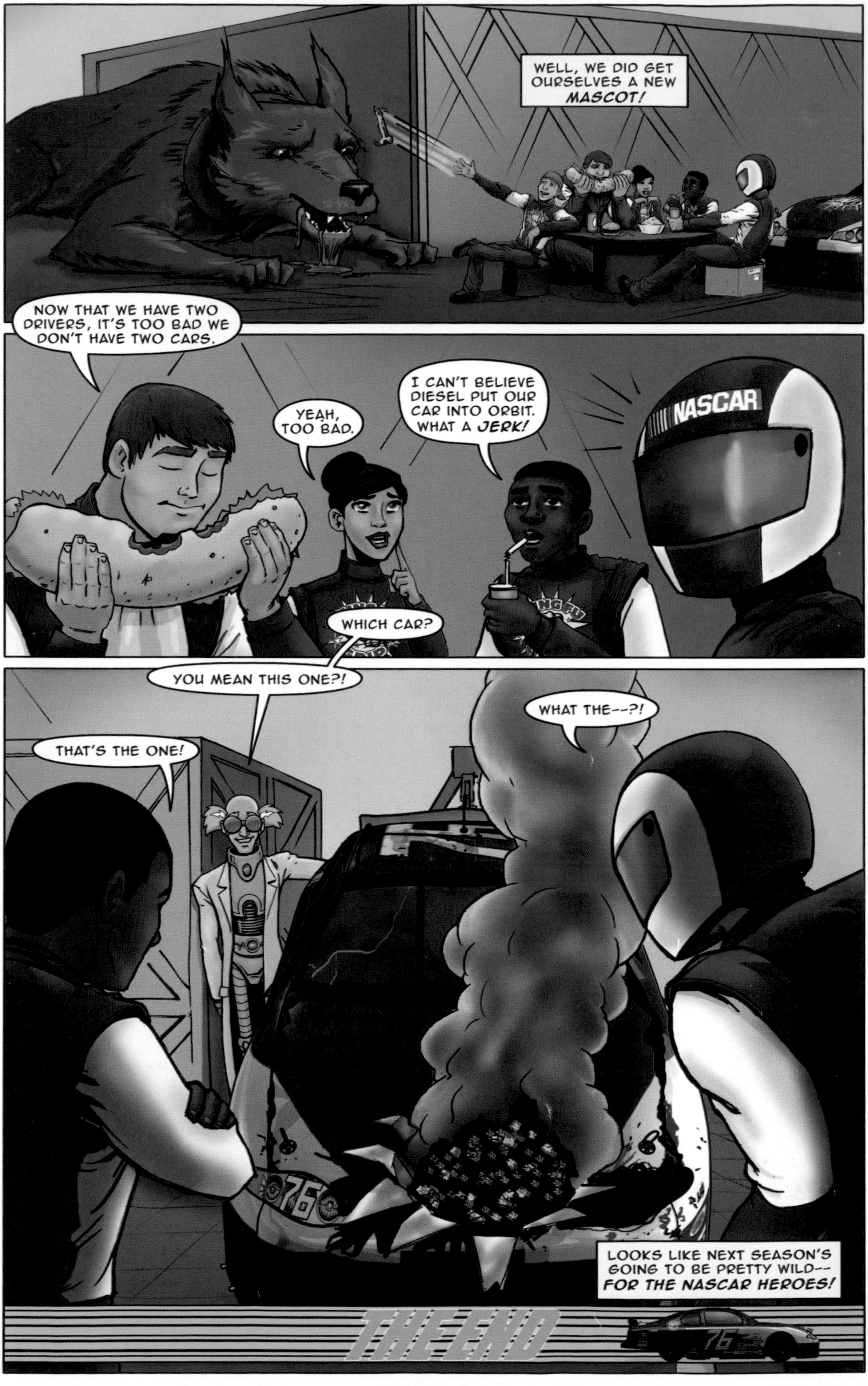
WELL, WE DID GET OURSELVES A NEW MASCOT!
NOW THAT WE HAVE TWO DRIVERS, IT'S TOO BAD WE DON'T HAVE TWO CARS.
YEAH, TOO BAD.
I CAN'T BELIEVE DIESEL PUT OUR CAR INTO ORBIT. WHAT A JERK!
NASCAR
WHICH CAR?
YOU MEAN THIS ONE?!
WHAT THE--?!
THAT'S THE ONE!
LOOKS LIKE NEXT SEASON'S GOING TO BE PRETTY WILD-- FOR THE NASCAR HEROES!
THE END

HOW TO DRAW
JIMMY DASH

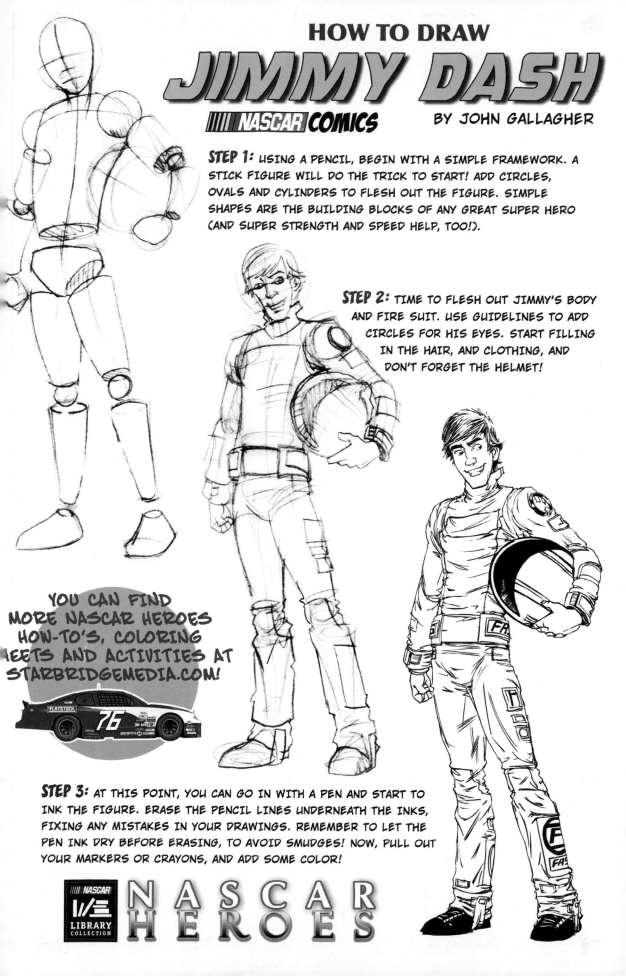

NASCAR COMICS

BY JOHN GALLAGHER

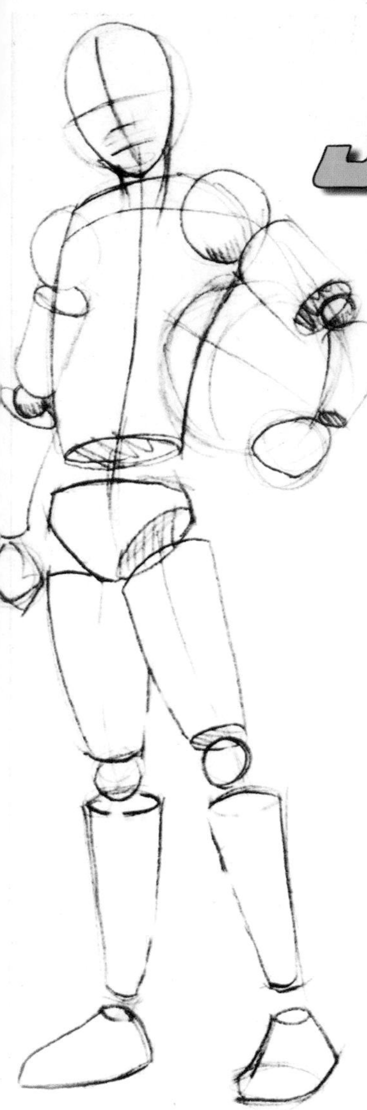

STEP 1: USING A PENCIL, BEGIN WITH A SIMPLE FRAMEWORK. A STICK FIGURE WILL DO THE TRICK TO START! ADD CIRCLES, OVALS AND CYLINDERS TO FLESH OUT THE FIGURE. SIMPLE SHAPES ARE THE BUILDING BLOCKS OF ANY GREAT SUPER HERO (AND SUPER STRENGTH AND SPEED HELP, TOO!).

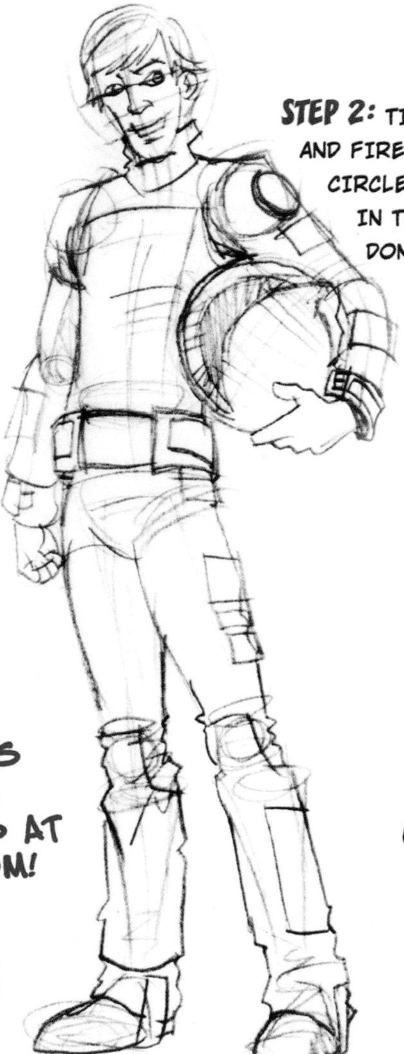

STEP 2: TIME TO FLESH OUT JIMMY'S BODY AND FIRE SUIT. USE GUIDELINES TO ADD CIRCLES FOR HIS EYES. START FILLING IN THE HAIR, AND CLOTHING, AND DON'T FORGET THE HELMET!

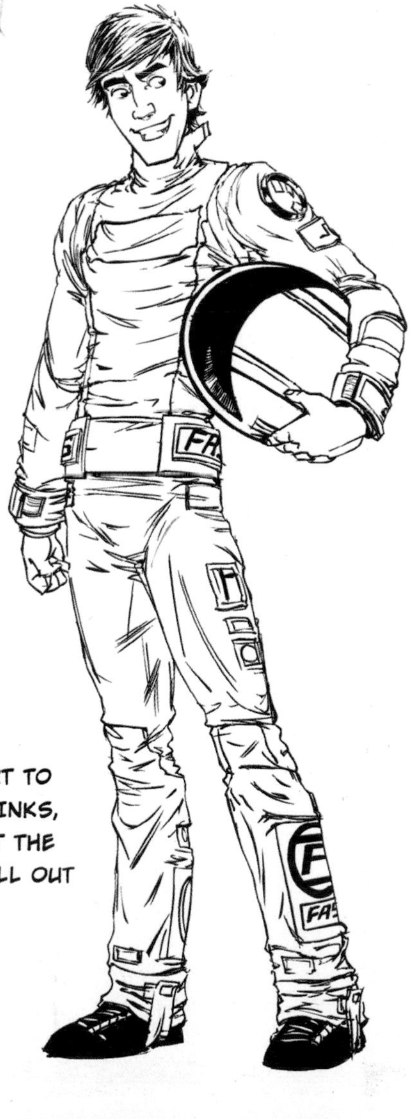

YOU CAN FIND MORE NASCAR HEROES HOW-TO'S, COLORING IEETS AND ACTIVITIES AT STARBRIDGEMEDIA.COM!

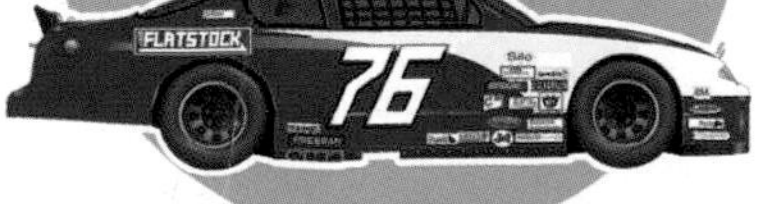
FLATSTOCK
76

STEP 3: AT THIS POINT, YOU CAN GO IN WITH A PEN AND START TO INK THE FIGURE. ERASE THE PENCIL LINES UNDERNEATH THE INKS, FIXING ANY MISTAKES IN YOUR DRAWINGS. REMEMBER TO LET THE PEN INK DRY BEFORE ERASING, TO AVOID SMUDGES! NOW, PULL OUT YOUR MARKERS OR CRAYONS, AND ADD SOME COLOR!

NASCAR LIBRARY COLLECTION

NASCAR HEROES

HOW TO DRAW NASCAR COMICS

JACK DIESEL'S NO. 63

BY JOHN GALLAGHER

SURE, JACK DIESEL'S A BAD GUY, BUT HE'S GOT A SET OF WHEELS THAT MAKE HIM A NASCAR SUPERSTAR! HERE'S A QUICK GUIDE ON HOW YOU CAN DRAW JACK'S RIDE!

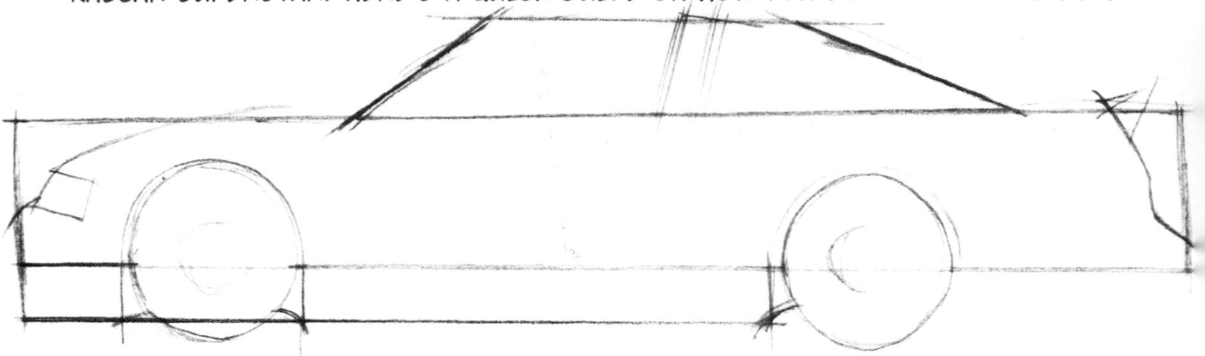

STEP 1: START OFF BY DRAWING A SERIES OF BOXES, SUGGESTING THE SHAPE OF THE CAR AND TIRES. IT'S LIKE CREATING A SHAPE WITH BUILDING BLOCKS, THEN CARVING AWAY AT THE SHAPE INSIDE. YOU CAN DO THIS FREEHAND, OR WITH A RULER, DEPENDING ON HOW "TIGHT" YOU WANT YOUR DRAWING!

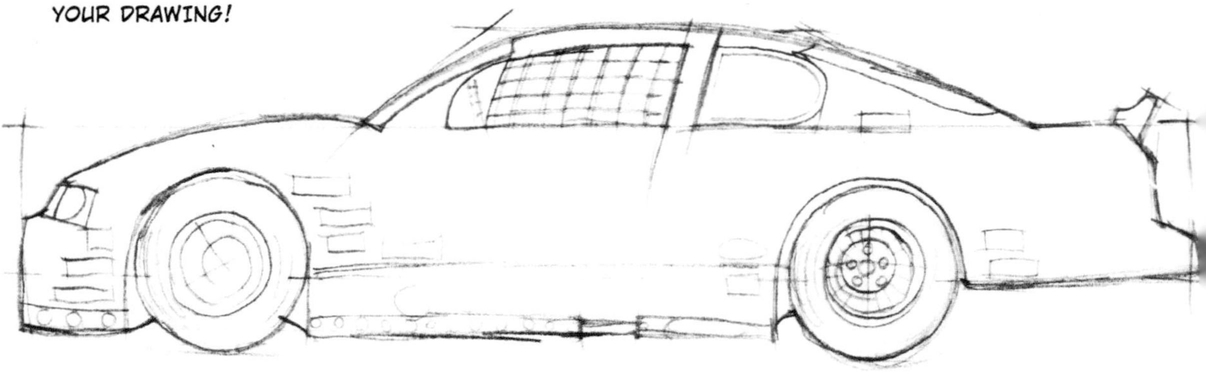

STEP 2: NOW, START TO ZERO IN ON THE SHAPE OF THE CAR FRONT, WINDOWS, TIRES, AND REAR SPOILER. THEN, YOU'LL WANT TO ADD THE DETAILS THAT MAKE A NASCAR UNIQUE, LIKE DECALS, NUMBERS, AND RIVETS!

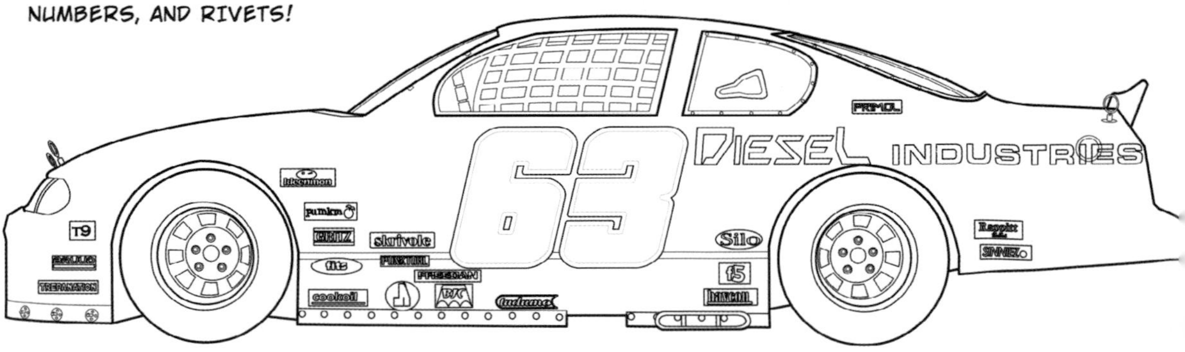
63
DIESEL
INDUSTRIES
T9
Silo
f5

STEP 3: AT THIS POINT, YOU CAN GO IN WITH A PEN AND START TO INK THE CAR, REALLY SHARPENING THE IMAGE! ERASE THE PENCIL LINES UNDERNEATH THE INKS, FIXING ANY MISTAKES IN YOUR DRAWING. GIVE THE CAR THE NUMBER OF YOUR FAVORITE DRIVE (BUT DON'T TELL JACK!), AND ADD SOME COLOR! NOW YOUR DRAWING IS READY TO RACE!

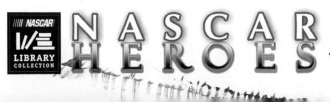